THE MURDER BUREAU

THE MURDER BUREAU

A Novel

By
Ron Kase

Library of Congress Control Number: 2020915187

ISBN: 9798649669054 – Paperback

Printed in the United States of America

A Series31 Book
Anchor Publishing

anchorpublishing31@gmail.com

You can always depend on Americans to do the right thing once they exhausted all other responsibilities.
Winston Churchill

The problem of human rights is so universal that it transcends all other problems that face humanity.
Fr. Theodore Hesburgh, CHC

Acknowledgements

Almost like the great Beatles' song, *With a Little Help from My Friends*, I actually had lots of help from my friends. The early readers of *The Murder Bureau* were Alice Pianfetti, Michael Riff and Carl Kraus who are among the smartest people I know. Since they liked the story, its timeliness, and actual possibility I was encouraged to keep writing and expanding the novel, and that's what I did. Once the manuscript was completed, as least I believed it was completed, I turned it over to Professor Keith O'Neil a careful and creative editor. Keith, a fiction writer himself, cleared up the rough spots, made the tenses agree, and corrected the errors that Spell Check missed. I'm grateful he was so exacting and envy Keith's students who learn about literature and language in his classes.

My good friend and fraternity brother, Saul Fern, introduced me to the scientific article describing the ancient Picts people who inhabited the settlement Skara Brae located in the Orkney Islands of Northern Scotland. The Picts people existed in the harsh northern region for over 1200 years from about 2500 BCE. Their history is the basis of Dr. Kavanagh's thesis found in *The Murder Bureau* and previously in my novel *Kavanagh's Dilemma*.

I'm grateful to the seven days a week continuing coverage of Donald Trump's crimes and hideous behavior as reported by *The New York Times, Washington Post,* MSNBC and CNN.

Once again, I am grateful to *The Auden Trust* for its continuing support.

INTRODUCTION

This is a tale, a fantasy of what may become a solution to some of the havoc caused by Donald J. Trump, the 45th President of the United States while he was in office. Often referred to as the most unprepared person in the nation's history to be a president, Trump nevertheless garnered undying support from about one third of Americans. His appeal to them was his ignorant, racist, nativist approach to immigration from Latin America. His tolerance of white supremacists added to Trump's credibility among the underemployed citizens who inhabit the rust belt and the Old South. Trump also found support from the leaders of corporations that produced coal, chemicals, and other polluting agents who welcomed the lifting of environmental regulations.

In 2022, a newly elected president, desperate to re-assemble the nation's infrastructure that was destroyed by Trump, convenes a secret panel of diverse people. Their assignment is the evaluation of those who are attempting to extend the Trump legacy with a fascist type government as their desired result. The secret panel becomes known among its six members as The Murder Bureau.

A member of the panel, Lydia Merriman, the talented and beautiful African-American woman who after a spectacular quarter century career with Ted Turner's influential media company has become the representative from New York's 18th congressional district. Lydia was introduced to readers in the earlier novel *"Kavanagh's Dilemma."* Dr. Kavanagh, the academic from that story, remains hopelessly in love with Lydia and once again becomes intricately involved in her personal and then her political life during the post vulgar Trump time that continues after he is defeated.

"The Murder Bureau" is a "future fantasy," which of course can never happen, but will it need to?

CHAPTER 1

The White House, February 6, 2022

Pennsylvania Avenue as usual was filled with slow moving traffic. The Congresswoman in the taxi's back seat was becoming nervous and fidgety, which was highly unusual for her as she was known for her cool nature and confident demeanor. However this day she was on her way for a 10 am appointment in the White House with the President. The time was 9:55 when the taxi escaped from the choking traffic and drove to the guard booth, the first barrier of the President's residence and office. Showing her congressional credentials, the Congresswoman hopped from the taxi and was spotted by a young woman, a presidential aide, sent to find her at the building's official visitor's entrance. Whisked inside the White House, the representative of New York's 18th Congressional District hurried to the Oval Office and was ushered inside.

Before she could get an apology out for being tardy, the smiling President greeted her. "Lydia Merriman, how long has it been since I was a guest on your TV show in Atlanta?"

"I don't know, maybe ten years, and I'm flattered you remembered considering how many appearances you make."

The President had won the 2020 election with a landslide victory repudiating the personal and political excesses of Donald J. Trump the disgraced fascist loving, criminal, megalomaniac who had brought the nation to the brink of its losing the essence of the Constitution and what it has stood for and protected for over two hundred and forty years. He didn't recover from the impeachment, and his actions became even crazier, and even more incompetent especially related to the Covid-19 pandemic. Over two hundred thousand Americans died because of Trump's criminal negligence. Republicans just looked on and blamed Nancy Pelosi since blaming Barack Obama and Hillary no longer had currency.

However, presently the senate was still under Republican control with a 51 – 49 majority. It was due to the lackluster performance of Democrats who didn't sufficiently challenge Republican incumbents in the senate races because twenty three of them actually had presidential pretenses. Almost two dozen Democrats announced their campaigns for the presidency, and formally good candidates in possible swing states stayed on the sidelines watching to see the way the elections would turn out while estimating their own chances for future success in politics.

"I'm sure you're curious why I asked you here this morning." The President motioned for Lydia to sit on the couch across from the famous *Resolute* desk, a gift from Queen Victoria to Rutherford B. Hayes and took the chair perpendicular to her. "Defeating Trump was just the beginning. We have to restore alliances with foreign countries that had taken decades to create and were destroyed in an instant because of Trumps personal business interests.

We have had to rehabilitate the State Department, HUD, the Treasury, Homeland Security, Education, Commerce and Labor because the people appointed to run the departments were either incompetent or criminal or both. The FBI and the NSA are being restored to their former proper positions, but it all takes time and careful planning. It's only been a year, however, the Southern border's concentration camps have been dismantled, and American's have contributed extraordinary amounts of humanitarian aid to the people stuck there, some for three years." The President's eyes were watery and Lydia was reminded of the tragedies faced by the nation's leader every day.

Lydia began, "I can assure you that the House with its seventy member Democratic majority is doing everything it can, but until we win in the Senate, we're frustrated." As she said this, Lydia wondered why she, a second term congresswoman, was discussing national policy privately with the President of the United States. An actual president quite unlike the Trump circus clown who had devalued the office.

The President rose, walked to a window and looked out to the perfectly tended green lawn. Turning back, showed a sad smile, and sat down again. "I'm sure you realize that Trump opened up the worst of some American's fears, and made it all right to act on them. He encouraged division and hate of black and brown people. He let gun organizations, far right hate groups, nativists and white evangelicals act out their disdain for anyone who didn't fit into their model of America where everyone looks alike.

It's almost as if he studied Hitler's *Mein Kamph* except we all knew Trump read on a fourth grade level." The President stopped speaking and poured a glass of water from a carafe on the coffee table near Lydia. Motioning to her, offering to fill another glass, but she declined. "Trump used the resurgence of Populism here and in Europe to attract the anti-intellectual, anti-elite as supporters, and they stayed with him no matter how bizarre his behavior became. In fact, George Will called Populism, lawlessness in the service of curdled envy and resentment."

Lydia declared, "With Trump out of office won't this all settle down and return to what was considered normal?" She hesitated, but went on. "Look as a black woman, I don't expect much from my fellow Americans. Sure there's been progress, but as soon as Trump said it was all right too openly hate, the Klan and other bigots came out from under the rocks where they had been hiding."

The President shook his head. "No I don't think it will get much better for a while. Possibly not for a long while and we don't have the time as a nation to deal with it though education and speeches. In reality, the South won the civil war, and has controlled the national dialogue in regard to race relations, civil rights, voter access, gun ownership and limiting labor unions. There's a well-financed far right network out there doing damage every day to basic rights and the environment. And it's not about Trump, not any more. He has plenty of trouble with banks foreclosing on his properties, New York State prosecuting him for bank fraud, and money laundering, the divorce revealing his low net worth, income tax evasion charges and Trump hotels targets for terrorists."

"In fact I believe he's moved out of Trump Tower in New York because it became a ghost town with eighty percent of the Russian and Saudi owned apartments abandoned, and Deutsche Bank foreclosing on the rest. Also he lost Mara Largo in Florida. A joint project of the Cleveland Clinic and the Hospital for Special Surgery will demolish the buildings and create a world class center for health care."

Lydia, as a congresswoman from New York's 18th Congressional District, was aware of the legal actions being brought against Trump by various regulatory agencies and the state's Attorney General. "I know about some of Trump's troubles, and it's good he's been neutralized. It took impeachment and the tragedy of the Coronavirus to wake up Americans to the threat of his criminality and gross incompetence."

The President agreed. "Yes, but there are too many dangerous people who influence a great number of other people, and they have to be dealt with before it's too late. Before we see armed insurrection in our streets," which he said with passion. After hesitating for a long moment he said, "And of course you're aware of the damage the Republican leadership in the Senate is doing arm-in- arm with the ARA. It's actually escalating. Do you remember the ARA making Trump declare gun stores essential businesses so they could stay open during the Covid-19 pandemic?" With eyes closed for a moment, the President turned to face Lydia directly and said, "I need your help."

CHAPTER 2

Knox College, Galesburg, Illinois, March 8, 2022

Galesburg, Illinois is about two hundred miles from Chicago's O'Hare Airport. The drive to Galesburg goes along Route 290 west toward Moline, Illinois and continues south for thirty miles along the Iowa state line. Located in Galesburg is historic Knox College, a fine liberal arts school that draws motivated students primarily from the center of the country although almost every state and scores of other countries are represented on campus. The college was founded in 1837 as an institution opposed to slavery in all forms: physical, intellectual and religious, and was open to all.

That was the place Lydia Merriman was headed to on a bright November morning when her plane landed at O'Hare at 8:30 and after she selected a rental car. Her meeting was scheduled at 1'oclock and she had been advised to first pick up some lunch at one of the dozen fast food restaurants along the route to the college and then proceed to campus. Three weeks ago, Lydia received a birthday card in the mail. The address appeared to be hand written, but a careful inspection indicated that it had been computer applied. The card was a nice Hallmark costing $5.99. The price of greeting cards still surprised Lydia, but she was even more surprised because her birthday was January 2, nine months away. The card wasn't signed, but a printed note was folded inside.

Your attendance is expected at our first meeting on March 8 held at Knox College in Galesburg, Illinois at 1 pm in the Lincoln Room of "Old Main." Drive alone to Knox College, and leave all possessions in the rental car. Notebooks, iPads, cellular phones, wallets, pens, wristwatches and hand bags are prohibited. Food must be purchased and consumed prior to entering the building. Do not introduce yourself to other attendees. Rules of operation will be made up at the first meeting. If staying at a hotel prior or after the meeting. Do not stay near Galesburg.

DESTROY THIS NOTE

Wow, thought Lydia. What have I gotten myself into? She knew that so many good people were working hard to restore the nation's balance so that honest dissent could be heard and respected. No reasonable person encouraged armed rebellion that would tear at the lives of people who were targeted or were in the way. America had a sorry history of small rebellions that turned out badly for the people involved who were often black citizens or union workers striking for living wages and humane working conditions. Now it was the people on the other side that presented the threat to good order and safety. Once Trump accepted the degenerate behavior of white supremacists in Charlottesville, Virginia the door opened and every hate group added to their membership. Prominent individuals, previously connected to Trump now roamed the land attracting followers who planned their version of jihad and pledged to destroy America in order to save it for white evangelical Christians, the *real* Americans.

Lunch consisted of strawberry yogurt and coffee. As Lydia drove to Knox College's campus, she saw that Galesburg was a typical small mid-western city. There was the main shopping street, schools, municipal buildings, private homes and the college. Galesburg's streets were tree lined and the city was more like a neighborhood. She wondered what attracted students to this remote place, but then realized that so many excellent small colleges are located in quiet rural regions. Once on the campus, Lydia easily found "Old Main" the single surviving building from the time of the fifth Lincoln – Douglas debate held at Knox College in 1858.

As Lydia walked up the steps to the building's entrance it was precisely 1 pm. She followed signs to the Lincoln Conference Room and was suddenly in the presence of three others. Two men and another woman. They carefully looked each other over silently until two more men entered the large room. There were awkward nods and smiles exchanged and someone suggested they sit at the round table and get started.

Looking around the table, Lydia evaluated the others who were no doubt doing the same thing. Across from her sat a man around her own age wearing a dark blue jacket and a black golf shirt. What was unknown to everyone was that he was the individual the President first approached and was the organizer of the project. He was a thin aesthetic appearing man who was the president of a university in Scranton, Pennsylvania. Lydia dubbed him, the Professor. Next to him was a prosperous, in-charge appearing man wearing a cashmere sweater over a designer sport shirt. He was African-American so Lydia was particularly interested in who he was and how he became a part of their secret group.

She recalled a billionaire paying off the student loans for the entire graduating class of Morehead College of Atlanta in 2019. While she didn't know if he was the man who did that great generous act, she decided to call him, the Philanthropist. Sitting to Lydia's right was the other woman in the group. She looked familiar and Lydia believed she may be a leader in the fight to protect women's health and reproductive rights. It would make great sense to include her since the Supreme Court, with its far right majority, was poised to take up Roe v Wade once again. That was due to the dying breaths of the white evangelical movement adopted by the Republicans who had managed to get laws passed in the poorest states that forbid abortions. No thought was given to pre or post-natal care, pre-school programs or child care so parents may earn enough money to raise children in a safe and healthy environment. In Lydia's mind the woman next to her was, the Advocate.

The man Lydia had called, the Professor, spoke quietly. "We all know why we are here. I will convene the session this time, but will not do it again. No one is in charge." He opened a brown paper bag that had been on the table in front of him and removed an instrument that looked like a large cell phone.

"This is a law enforcement grade, bug, phone, and camera detector. I volunteer to bring it to our meetings. Now I'll suggest a few ground rules, but if you don't agree, please make your feelings known and we will vote to adopt or reject. Shall I go on?" There were nods and murmurs of agreement so he continued. "We will meet here again in three months from today. The college uses a three semester calendar so there will always be activity on the campus so we will not stand out. If you happen to recognize your fellow members somewhere else, do not acknowledge it. Also one among us, and I do not know who, is the contact to the people who will carry out our decisions. That person is the Zodiac." He hesitated before saying, "First we should decide the number of votes required for action to be taken against an individual. All votes are open. And with that suggestion, I am no longer convening this meeting." He smiled slightly and looked away from the group.

A man younger than the others sat on the Professor's left. He appeared scholarly and impatient. He reminded Lydia of the characters from the TV show *The Big Bang Theory* so she made his nickname, the Scientist. He spoke up. "I strongly believe that due to the seriousness of our mission and the awesome power we have, if we decide to use it, decisions to terminate a life should be unanimous." There he said it. Lydia was brought back to reality as if she had been doused with cold water. They were meeting in this obscure place in secret in order to have people killed. Indeed, they were a murder bureau.

A lively sometimes passionate discussion ensued that lasted for about an hour. Several proposals were put forth from a simple majority vote to all having to agree as was proposed by the Scientist. Finally after several rounds the group agreed that a vote of five would seal the fate of the subject under review. Two no votes would end the discussion and members could not abstain. Next they began, at first hesitantly, to put out names of individuals who in their opinion offered the greatest threat to the fragile democratic government that barely survived Trump's drive to push America into a suspension of the Constitution thereby making him president for life. Trump was too stupid to understand the gross ramifications of his attempt to end the American experiment, but the people who had attached themselves to him knew exactly what they were doing by easily manipulating the weak narcissistic president. It had become obvious and frightening that Trump himself would never have been able to conceive of the actions necessary to topple the common order and turn America into a banana republic, even though that was exactly what he believed he could do.

Once the Knox group became a little more comfortable with the discussion, names were ventured, former Trump assistant Steve Mellor, Alex Jones, Marjorie Dannenfelser, Eugene Meyer, Kelly Ann Conway, Joe Arpaio, the Senate majority leader, and with the group's complete support, the ARA leadership. Hesitant at first, they became involved and then listened carefully to the Silicon Valley type who sported a full beard, torn jeans, but it was obvious he was someone to be reckoned with when he made his recommendation. Lydia thought of him as the Hippie. But he was deadly serious as he precisely outlined the case against Steve Bannon who had oddly been connected to Trump and occupied a powerful position for a short time in the Trump White House.

"He's been all over Europe the last two years inciting the fascist element that didn't die off even after World War Two. They're everywhere, France, Germany of course and Italy for Christ sake. Those people didn't learn anything from their history." The Hippie hesitated a moment before continuing. "He'll go to England next and cause more havoc there. The Brits are still recovering from the decision to leave the European Union. Bannon is trying in his own words to change the world order. He claims to speak for the disenfranchised white Europeans who are threatened by immigrants as if anyone needs him to be involved."

The Philanthropist asked, "So you believe Bannon has the ability to influence enough people to be a danger to our democracy?"

"I do. Bannon has influenced the Poles and Hungarians to move to the far right and limit human rights. You would have thought they had enough of fascism from the Germans and Russians, but no they're at it again with Bannon's help."

A serious discussion ensued with most agreeing that Bannon was menacing, but was he just a disheveled drunk made well known by Trump or a harbinger of the tyranny that many, even some Americans, inexplicably wanted? Lydia despised Bannon, but she didn't join the conversation because she didn't want her personal loathing of him to color the group's decision. The Professor interjected by saying, "Look it has to be more than a subject being a horrible excuse for a human being like Sarah Sanders, Bill Barr, the Kadassians or Marjorie Taylor Greene, and perhaps they will be punished, but not by us." After everyone else vented, and Bannon's character, personality and his potential for destruction of the social order was torn to pieces, the Hippie asked for a vote. Suddenly the room became quiet as if the air had been removed from it as the members realized that they were going to make their first life or death decision. Quickly hands were raised and five of the six agreed that Bannon should be marked for attention and elimination. The single no vote was cast by the Scientist. Even faster was the vote that decided the fate of the Senate Majority Leader and the governing body of the ARA.

The members were informed that one of their number, the Zodiac, would act as the conduit to the ultra-secret private organization that would carry out the group's decisions. Lydia wondered about that. She wasn't the conduit so who had that role? Perhaps the others were thinking about that but right now there was other business to attend to as another name was dropped into the swirl of emotions and the heated discussion.

The Philanthropist quietly said, "Harry Shaughnessy of the Fox News stable must be dealt with and soon. He commits crimes against the American people every time he opens his mouth on television. He's a racist clown who led the fiction that Barach Obama was born in Africa. Shaughnessy is a degenerate who has carried water for everyone who's against Obamacare, against increasing minimum wages, against women's choice and even against the social safety net. He continues to spread poison every night and his following is growing especially among the hate groups and their admirers even though they're the people who will be most disadvantaged." He stopped speaking and looked at each of the members. "The Klan and every other white supremacist group gain their energy from him. He not so subtly enjoys their attention and could become a demagogue attracting admirers from the evangelicals who yearn for a bleached white America. I'm asking for a vote now." Without any more discussion, hands were raised around the table, and Shaughnessy lost six to zero.

CHAPTER 3

Louisville, Kentucky April 3, 2022

The Gene Snyder U.S. Courthouse and Custom House is a massive early 20th Century six story office building located at 601 West Broadway in Louisville, Kentucky. Along with court rooms, judges' chambers and a dozen federal agencies are the offices of the Majority Leader of the United States Senate. The grizzled politician who has held the Senate in his clawed hands for over twenty years had strengthened the right wing agenda more effectively than any other elected official in the nation's history.

This morning, the leader was at the massive desk deep inside his office complex that occupied almost half of the Snyder Building's sixth floor. At exactly 10 o'clock two men dressed in dark suits, well-fitting button down white shirts and stripped ties showed their credentials to first a receptionist, then an assistant and finally to the deputy chief of staff. The men were FBI agents Samuel Collins and Rafael Reyes and they were there to see the Senate Majority Leader.

The deputy chief of staff was obviously unimpressed and informed the agents that without an appointment and a written request outlining their mission it was impossible to see the Senator as that was the office's protocol. The agents, used to dealing with insufferable fools, informed the deputy that they had come from Washington and what they had to convey in person to the Senator was more important than whatever protocol was in place, and that they might charge the deputy with interfering with a criminal investigation if they were not immediately admitted to the Senator's office. They were told to wait and after ten minutes were ushered into the inner sanctum. Once in the room, which was long and wide with three high windows and the Senator's aircraft carrier style desk in the center, the agents produced their credentials for the Senator's inspection.

After looking at their identification cards and photos and then carefully comparing them to each agent, the Senator looked at Rafael Reyes while saying in his nasal voice that had been likened to a bull frog choking, "I see the FBI has widened its net for recruiting, which isn't surprising considering the Bureau's sorry condition since it opposed Trump."

The FBI had been the target of both Democrats and Republicans since Director James Comey's bizarre announcement of his opinion of wrong doing by Hillary Clinton in the closing days of the 2016 presidential election. Criticized by many as being as detrimental to Clinton as Bernie Sanders' staying in the race to the bitter end, which gave the presidency to the most unlikely and unprepared person in America's history.

Once in office Trump fired Comey because the FBI Director would not engage in further illegal behavior Trump had requested in regard to overlooking the crimes of General Michael Flynn. Flynn, who no doubt was compromised by the Russian government, and was unbelievably Trump's advisor on national security, created a situation that previously would only be found in an *Animal House* genre movie. Peter Strzok an FBI Special Agent and a leader of the Bureau's Counter Intelligence Unit was also fired for sending anti-Trump emails foolishly on his office computer to an associate Lisa Page, an FBI lawyer who was also forced out of the Bureau. And finally Deputy Director Andrew McCabe's career was terminated shortly before his date of retirement because he questioned the unlikely number of Russian/Trump contacts and criticized Trump's "relentless attack of the FBI." Trump fired McCabe as a warning to all federal staffers that his actions were not to be questioned thus completing the FBI purge, which was approved by a Republican congress.

Reyes startled said, "Pardon me Senator, I don't understand your comment."

"I believe you do understand me. Now what do you two want? I don't enjoy people from Washington dropping in without being cleared for an appointment in advance. Do you actually believe I have time to see just anyone who decides to come by?" He was in character as the guardian of extreme right wing dogma, and had survived the Mueller Report era through stockpiling millions of campaign dollars from billionaire casually fascist backers who opposed anything be it medical coverage or even Social Security benefiting the poor or even working class Americans. The Senator's net worth topped $13 million, which considering that the annual salary of a United States Senator is $174,000 and that residing in Washington, DC was one of the nation's most expensive places to live, he has done remarkably well growing a modest salary into a respectable monetary fund without lifting a finger outside of the Senate.

Collins approached the desk and said, "I'm going to tell you why we're here. Of course it has to be treated as completely confidential. That's the reason the director sent us to see you in person." Having explained their mission, Collins walked directly to the Senator, leaned over him as if to whisper in his ear, except he suddenly put his hand on the Senator's right temple and his other hand under the Senator's jaw on the opposite side, and quickly snapped the majority leader's neck. The Senator's eyes rolled back in his head, his mouth open as if to scream, but no sound was heard.

Agent Reyes now wearing plastic gloves had opened one of the office's large windows. He picked up the unconscious Senator with help from Collins, brought him to the window and threw him out. The window was left open and the agents left the office first snapping the button of the lock on the door's spine. Collins spoke to the legislative assistant stationed in the outer office. "The Senator asks for ten minutes to deal with the information we brought him. He doesn't want to see anyone."

They thanked the receptionist, walked out to the main corridor and split up taking separate flights of stairs to the first floor and exits to the street. Sirens were starting to fill the air. People rushed toward the Snyder Federal Building. Collins and Reyes who hadn't seen each other before they killed the Senator destroyed their FBI credentials which were excellent forgeries, and never saw each other again.

CHAPTER 4

May 8, 2022, Indianapolis, Indiana

The Indiana Convention Center once again welcomed the acres of deadly weapons and related items guaranteed to cause bloody mayhem when purchased and used by American terrorists. It was the 151st Annual Convention of the American Rifle Association the lobbying organization for gun manufacturers that sell billions of dollars of deadly war weapons to ordinary Americans whose masturbatory fantasies involve embracing assault rifles. Streams of campers poured into the camp grounds around the city. The great unwashed originating primarily from the fly-over states waited all year between conventions to breathe in the atmosphere of the exhibit floor where real men could talk about guns and ammo with other real men.

The three day event also offered, for an extra charge, seminars useful to American gun owners in the 21st Century. They signed up to, "Methods of Concealed Carry," "The Science of Draw Time," and "Armed Citizen – How to Interact with Law Enforcement." All reinforcing gun owners their right to cause mayhem and deadly damage as they believe was guaranteed by the Second Amendment.

The election of members to the ARA's board of directors was also held at this time. The board consists of seventy-six patriotic gun enthusiasts with twenty-five elected each year for three year terms. Many board members are simply wealthy right wingers.

The TV actor and reverse mortgage huckster who had a new career cheating elderly people out of their homes has been on the board for about thirty years, Ted Nugent the talentless singer, draft dodger, anti-Semite, hater of blacks and other minorities is also a long-time board member as was the disgraced Colonel Ollie North of Iran-Contra fame, a convicted felon who was deposed as ARA president in 2019. Another of the glorious tribe representing "Making American Great Again" is Allan West, former Republican congressman and a convicted war criminal during George W. Bush's war on Iraq, who was actually president of the ARA for a while until he challenged ARA czar Wilson DePeters' spending for clothing and other personal items that added up to hundreds of thousands of ARA dollars.

The real business of the ARA, money laundering, passing on Russian money to Republican politicians and lobbying Congress to prevent passing laws that limit in any manner gun ownership, is overseen by a sinister border line personality individual. He had, for thirty years, convinced even non-gun owners that the U.S. Constitution guarantees all sociopaths and psychopaths the right to gun ownership. That it is the inalienable right of anyone, even if you're a criminal and your name appears on the no-fly list, to own assault weapons and human organ destroying ammunition. The ARA's long time executive director is Wilson DePeters who has held the organization tightly in his fist for decades. Once considered a simpleton, a harmless looser from upstate New York, DePeters has parlayed his brand of hate, fear of government, and the lack of education and ambition exhibited by the typical ARA member into a cash generating machine.

DePeters' outrageous defense of gun ownership at all costs had become an expected follow up to tragic events that galvanized the nation after the devastatingly painful Columbine High School massacre of teenagers in Colorado in 1999. That had followed the heart wrenching campus mass murder spree that was notoriously mismanaged at Virginia Tech University in 2007. After each unbelievably tragic event, DePeters bravely stood his ground in front of TV cameras assuring Americans that, "Guns don't kill people, people kill people," his logic twisted by a corroded syphilitic type damaged brain and inability to feel empathy or sympathy resulted in encouraging the simple minded members of the public to acquire even more deadly armaments after each of the mass murders enacted at schools, colleges, and other places where innocent people gathered.

However, DePeters hit a low point that was previously unimagined by a civil society in the 21st Century when he again defended combat type armament sales to ordinary people after the most unspeakable tragedy in modern American history the systematic murder of elementary school children, babies really, in Sandy Hook, Connecticut in 2012. President Barack Obama came to Sandy Hook immediately after the events of the worst day unfolded. He promised the grieving parents and nearly hysterical teachers who believed they had failed their students even though six of their number had also been murdered that day that laws preventing this great American tragedy from happening again would be passed. The ARA and its public relations firm, Ackerman McQueen that receives millions annually from the gun rights organization geared up a campaign telling the nation that guns were not to blame. It was the lack of mental health screening and treatment of persons who might carry out this kind of act. And incidentally, they proclaimed, and were believed, that the Eastern liberals and intellectuals and the black president were the problem as they wanted to take away guns from everyone. Of course the complete lack of logic of that claim didn't bother the gun nuts who quickly stocked up by buying assault rifles in record numbers causing DePeters to say to that the president was the best salesman for their deadly products.

Again in 2018 when another deadly murder spree took place in a school, DePeters tried to justify gun ownership by any murderous individual. The high school in Parkland, Florida was the scene of bloody carnage inflicted by just one murderer. This time DePeters was helped in the "Guns are not the problem" campaign automatically flooding the media by an attractive dark haired woman called Diana Lee Leech. Leech, a mother of two boys had no reluctance to demand that the Second Amendment be honored without any consideration of the butchery that has gone on because of the ignorant belief that the nation's Founders actually wanted everyone to own guns, and after two centuries there was no reason to change that belief. After the Parkland High School killings, Leech was all over television especially Fox News coldly calling gun owners the victims rather than the students whose lives were brutally cut short in their own high school. Apparently Leech, who was paid over a $1 million annually, would have the same attitude toward deadly assault weapons even if her own children were murdered.

DePeters wasn't on the exhibition floor. He stayed away from the ARA's membership if he could avoid them. He mostly remained in his suite on the ninth floor of the Westin Indianapolis Hotel an upscale place that was attached to the convention center by a skyway. The hotel's executive suite contained two bedroom, three bathrooms and a large living room with a conference table in its center. He was in a bedroom talking on the phone to the little Republican senator from Florida who was demanding additional money from the ARA for the fight against a powerfully funded opponent in the upcoming election. The Democratic candidate was a woman of Puerto Rican origin, a marine scientist at the University of Tampa. "Tampa," muttered DePeters, "another god dam liberal swamp." He was clearly frustrated by the encroachment of intelligent people who were not interested in the Second Amendment or in owing a gun.

Meanwhile in the suite's living room the seven most influential members of the ARA's board of directors were listening to and watching Diana Leech present the organization's plans for influencing media outlets in the coming year. Her message was, "get tougher, or lose your guns." The board members, all men, were enjoying Leech's performance as she wore a short black dress that hugged her shapely body and high heel black pumps that emphasized the movements of her hips. Just a few years ago a suggestive poster showing a side view of Leech wearing a clingy red dress, four inch high heels and holding an assault rifle was sold out as soon as it was offered to the ARA membership. The poster's message along with Leech's sexuality was "Hands off my Gun," with a sub title, "Defeating the Plot to Disarm America."

DePeters knew he had to go back to the board members. The ARA's new president was a former Mississippi Republican congressman. Another "genius" DePeters thought dismissively. He remembered when a legendary movie star was the organization's president. The PR firm Ackerman McQueen came up with the slogan, "You will have to pry my gun from my cold dead hands." The actor actually thought he said it first and it was identified with him for the rest of his life. "Jesus, how do I stand these people?" DePeters couldn't help thinking about Ollie North, the disgraced and convicted Army colonel who became a sweetheart of the far-right wingers and ultimately was elected president of the ARA. In 2019, Ollie North tried to unseat the ARA leadership accusing them of gross financial improprieties. Of course, DePeters won out and, North resigned.

DePeters opened the bedroom's door watching Diana Leech for a moment. He noticed that waiters were setting up a luncheon spread along one wall of the living room. The food, beer and liquor bottles were being transferred to tables covered with white clothes. DePeters was curious because he hadn't asked for lunch to be served in the suite in fact he believed a lunch reservation for the group had been made in the hotel's restaurant called Nourish off of the lobby. DePeters standing in the door way signaled for a waiter to come to talk to him. The waiter, a man of average height with light colored hair approached him, and when DePeters began to speak, he suddenly wasn't able to get out any words because he had been shot twice in his head by the waiter using a Heckler & Koch 9mm pistol with a silencer.

As DePeters fell to the floor the three waiters turned on the board members and Diana Leech killing all of them in about ten seconds. Making sure all were dead, the waiters loaded up one cart with sandwiches and a pail of imported beer, then closed the door to the living room before opening the suites' main door. Rolling the cart out to the corridor, the waiters told the security team stationed at the suite's entrance that DePeters sent the food and beer out to them. The security team was grateful and flattered. They were asked to bring the cart to the service elevator after the food was consumed. They happily agreed, and the waiters took off in the direction of the service area. They took the stairs to the fifth floor and entered a room using a hotel card. Without a word uttered among them, the waiters transformed themselves to other identities. One now wore a dark suit, white shirt and necktie. Another overalls with a local HVAC company's logo on his back, and the other man had donned a sport shirt and zippered jacket with an ARA Convention sticker on his left chest. Wigs were removed, eyebrows returned to their actual look and makeup that changed face complexion was cleaned away.

The waiters' outfits were loaded into a Westin Hotel trash bag and left in the room. Later a chamber maid would pick up the bag for careful disposal. The three Heckler & Koch pistols with silencers and extra rounds were placed in a briefcase with the logo of the Fidelity Investment firm, which was holding an event at the Westin Hotel that day. The briefcase was to be carried by the dark suited individual. The men exited the hotel room and took an elevator to the lobby splitting up and leaving the hotel by separate exits. The man carrying the briefcase got into a taxi at the hotel's front and directed the driver to take him to the Union Railroad Station located on South Illinois Street. The old historic building was the nation's first Union Station. The passenger left the taxi, entered the station and exited a few minutes later to a different street. He walked two blocks to Harry & Izzy's restaurant where he was seated at a table on the main floor. The briefcase holding the three pistols was placed on a chair across from the diner who ordered a St. Elmo shrimp cocktail and pan seared scallops along with a diet Coke. While he enjoyed the lunch, an attractive blond woman walked by his table. She carried a small brown suitcase. Without a word or a look exchanged the woman picked up the Fidelity Investment briefcase replacing it with the overnight bag. Paying the lunch check with cash, the man left the restaurant and hailed a cab for a ride to the Indianapolis Airport in plenty of time to make his direct flight to Paris for a two or three week stay or until the ARA story was no longer news.

CHAPTER 5

Fox News Studios, Manhattan, June 8, 2022

Four months after meeting with the President in the Oval Office, Lydia was grappling with the role she had been asked to assume in order to help bring back sanity to the nation after four years of Trump. Yes, she had agreed to become part of the project outlined by the President that day, and she had done what she was asked to do, but sleep evaded Lydia most nights as she fought with herself over the choice she made. The iPhone had beeped all night, but it was ignored. She was fearful of the messages she might see. Now at 7 am, Lydia didn't have any more choices, she had to read the news feeds from the *Times, Washington Post* and CNN.

Lydia was still loyal to CNN even after its sale to Time Warner and the disastrous combination of mismanagement and loss of mission that had resulted in CNN losing its prominence as the most viewed news network. She had a twenty three year career in Atlanta with Ted Turner, CNN's founder and all around business genius. Before leaving Atlanta in 2015, Lydia had been president of several television stations that were profit centers for Turner. Lydia's stock options made her wealthy and after moving to Millbrook, New York she became visible through generous support of local organizations that promoted women's health issues, homeless shelters, food pantries and a free health maintenance organization that served families living just above the level for

Medicaid eligibility. In 2020, Lydia campaigned as a Democrat to represent her district in Congress. She was swept into office along with the popular Democrat presidential candidate, and won re-election in 2022.

After reading the headlines and messages on her iPhone, Lydia went to her apartment's front door and picked up the *Washington Post and The New York Times*. The newspapers had the same headlines, more subdued on the *Times'* front page of course. The stories were all the same. About 10 o'clock last night at Fox News, 1211 Avenue of the Americas in New York City, the hate mongering conduit for Trump's lies and insults and assaults on the Constitution, their gray haired pompous, Trump enabler and chief commentator, was found hanged in his office by his feet in an imitation of Mussolini's death. His mouth, hands and ankles were taped and his face was even more grotesque after life than when he polluted television with crazy false and dangerous claims concerning Barack Obama, Hillary Clinton, gays, Muslims, Hispanic immigrants, climate change and the fictional "death panels" supposedly included in the Affordable Care Act. Lydia felt a chill, not because of Fox's pathological liar's death, but because she knew when he had been marked to die.

Lydia's conversation with the President had taken place almost a half year ago, nevertheless, it was burned into her memory. She was flattered when he asked for her help assuming it was connected with upcoming legislation, but still it was unusual for the occupant of the Oval Office to approach a second term member of congress so directly. Therefore Lydia was surprised when the President launched into an explanation of how Trump with extraordinary assistance from Attorney General Barr had come close to destroying the Constitution and the nation's delicate balance that ensured our democracy.

The President used an example to illustrate the point, Hitler and his rise from outsider to supreme leader of Germany. His assent to total control of that nation was aided by politicians and military leaders who felt their own positions were not secure so they threw in with a lunatic. Germany's Chancellor could have stopped Hitler, but didn't, much like the Republican leadership in the Senate that could have stopped Trump, but didn't. And the lunatic's rhetoric seduced the Germans much in the same manner as Trump's calls for stopping Mexican "rapists" at the border and certain Muslims, not Saudis however, from ever coming to the United States, captivated white rural crowds.

The people in the mining and industrial Great Plains states were under employed and under educated Americans. They are still waiting for the coal mines to open again so the ghost smokestacks of the industrial mid-west would again spill out thick black smoke. They were told over and again by Trump and his surrogates that "illegals were going to take their jobs." That America was becoming brown and that Spanish would become the nation's official language. Ridiculous, of course, but as the "left out" Americans saw many more black people on cable news programs, black people who were lawyers, professors, doctors, authors and cyber security experts, they believed that their very existence as real white Christian Americans was being threatened.

The President confided in Lydia that day regarding the existence of a Fifth Column poised to fight with violence against the imagined "Deep State." That was a threat developed primarily since Trump was defeated for a second term in a humiliating election. He raved about the election "being rigged" against him from election night until the inauguration in January where he actually attempted to speak in order to rally his invisible supporters among those honoring the new president thus marking the end of Trump's administration, and as Sinclair Lewis put it in 1935, the end of "The Revolt against Civilization."

While Trump himself wasn't a threat to democracy any longer, there were people in strategic positions who encouraged the divisive policies of Trump. Pitting Americans against other Americans worked for Trump, for a while. Gun ownership among non-sport gun owners sky rocketed under Trump. Spotlighting immigrants at the southern border as the nation's greatest threat worked for

Trump among some Americans. And while Trump was trying to put a life back together between court appearances and foreclosures on his properties, there were others quietly attempting to build a coalition with an agenda that promised to make America white and immigrant free again. They planned to accomplish their manifesto by stripping away the human rights of anyone who did not conform to the nativist and racist definition of the "ideal citizen." The tightening of America was set forth by the Koch brothers network of associations, the majority of Republicans, Fox News and the other emerging "news" networks that poisoned broadcast media and social networks with outrageous claims, outright lies and blatant encouragement of the self-radicalized who felt threatened and harassed by any form of social progress.

Lydia assured the President that as a member of the House Intelligence Committee she was quite aware of the threat from extremist groups that Trump had fertilized and tacitly supported by refusing to condemn them. And that the committee received reports on a regular basis from The Southern Poverty Law Center and the Anti-Defamation League. The President acknowledged the importance of the committee's work, but said, "We have to do more than watching."

"Lydia, I believe I can trust you. I've thought a great deal about what I'm going to say now. There are some people who pose a terrible threat to the Constitution. It's not new, but never before had they been encouraged by an entire presidential administration including the Attorney General. That went on for four years. I've been putting the government back together as fast as it's possible to do. It's not always easy or successful. Trump left a lot of poison pills in departments. Education is a mess, it's as if Betsy DeVos set out to destroy the sacred concept of compulsory education for all children. HUD is almost non-functioning since that idiot was appointed Secretary, and Labor is collapsing. The VA must be completely re-established. Actually I would like to see the VA under the Pentagon. It just doesn't make sense that the VA is run by civilians. As you know, I've travelled to every one of our allies, and then to the places that are not our friends. I had to tell all of them in person that the America they knew before Trump is back in business."

Lydia wondered where this was going, and she soon found out. The President continued. "A great deal of money was secretly contributed by a popular billionaire to set up an organization, a very small, very secret organization, to deal effectively with those people who are leading efforts to undermine the Constitution. I have asked five other people, and you are the sixth, to become the decision makers in regard to whom attention must be paid in order to stop the poison they spread, which can't be dealt with effectively through law enforcement and the courts."

"When you say attention must be paid," she had asked, "what do you mean?"

"Unfortunately that means after due deliberation," the President had said that day," the individuals marked for attention by the group or bureau or whatever you all decide to be, well they will be permanently eliminated."

Lydia had to be sure. "Do you mean killed?" The President just nodded.

CHAPTER 6

Washington, DC

Washington, DC is known as The District, and the District is a collection of neighborhoods that once were autonomous and separate in status and economic level. In recent years the neighborhoods one by one became gentrified, expensive and home to the educated professionals working for the government and for the hundreds of foundations, think tanks, research centers and the associations established to lobby congress day after day until the laws they wanted were passed and the regulations they didn't want were dropped.

The District's most diverse neighborhood is Columbia Heights in the North West section of the city, which no longer has affordable housing except through government programs for low income families. The blocks of beige brick three story attached houses with pointed roofs were built just after the Civil War for prominent families. As time went on the buildings were divided into separate apartments housing multiple families. That was over thirty years ago before the Heights became one of the District's most desirable places to reside. Upon her election to Congress in 2020, Lydia found a *pied-a-terre* that shared the second floor of a townhouse on 13th Street NW. She lived quietly and alone during her first term. Upon being re-elected, Lydia thought about finding a more permanent place to live. She wanted additional space and views of the busy street rather than the garages in the alley her rented apartment windows overlooked. On a Saturday in late January, she hurried along her street to escape from the cold. Lydia had decided to walk from the Safeway market about a half mile from her home, and even the one bag of food and paper products was proving to be a burden. As she hurried up the block, Lydia noticed a For Sale sign being put up just two doors from her place. After going home to drop off the groceries, Lydia went back outside, copied down the real estate agent's name and phone number and called.

The agent, new in the office, didn't know that the sign had already been placed on the small square of a front lawn. An hour later she and Lydia met up and after a tour of the building's three floors, two of which were floor through finished apartments with new kitchens and baths, oak floors and bay windows, Lydia, surprising the agent, agreed to buy the building for the asking price. She was able to purchase the building quickly because during her twenty three year career at Turner Broadcasting she had collected stock, due to Ted Turner's generosity, in the corporation that was worth $13 million when the company was sold to Time Warner.

Following the advice of some of the business insiders she became acquainted with during her time as a Turner executive, Lydia immediately sold the Time Warner shares and invested in U.S. Treasury Bills for the short term. Heeding more advice, Lydia in 2013 invested in Amazon, Lennar, Toll Brothers and Facebook. The original nest egg turned into $19 million, which has been converted to safe conservative investments in public utilities, municipal bonds and steady slow growth mutual funds.

Lydia had built her congressional staff carefully. Each member of congress is entitled to employ a staff of eighteen. Lydia's staff in her third year in Congress totaled fourteen. Her office in the Rayburn Office Building on Capitol Hill housed eight staff members and herself. She inherited three from her predecessor and recruited a legislative assistant, the most significant staffer, who had worked for the legendary Nancy Pelosi, and was strongly recommended to Lydia by the Speaker. For her chief of staff, the person who oversaw all of the office's operations, Lydia was fortunate to connect with Grace Ellen Hill. Hill was a tireless and competent individual who had been a member of the Obama administration.

Secure that there were five people in the office who actually knew what to do, Lydia recruited the others from her district in New York. Two young women who hailed from Dutchess County had become lawyers. One graduated from Cardozo School of Law, and was an assistant district attorney in White Plains, New York, and the other from NYU Law School was counsel to New York City's comptroller. They became her writers of drafts, memos and responses. The last to be hired were two constituent relations specialists who knew the 18th Congressional District thoroughly, and were able to deal effectively with the requests for assistance that emerged daily in congressional offices. Lydia worked long hours dealing personally with as many issues as she was able to, and met regularly with her constituents who had come to Washington, while refusing the attention of lobbyists.

Two trips to *west elm* the home furnishing store near Logan Circle was all Lydia required in order to fill up her new floor through space. She selected area rugs, living room and dining room casual furniture, lamps and some decorative objects. The apartment's walls displayed paintings by her favorite contemporary African artists: Peju Alatise was a young woman whose oil paintings of African women captured their beauty, but also their mistrust of what their future might hold.

The work of Gopal Dagnogo was vibrant, and his use of colors was encompassing and held one's attention. Lydia also owned two paintings made by Cheri Samba that depicted modern African family life, a departure from the continents' usual artistic representation of native women dressed in traditional garb. The canvases, some large, had been packed and crated and shipped to Washington by art handlers. Two of her staff members helped hang the works in the new apartment. At a gallery near DuPont

Circle Lydia spotted and purchased a dazzling painting by Jennifer Packer a black American woman who had recently completed a master's degree in fine art at Yale. Packer painted expressionist portraits of average people going about their lives that the viewer could identify with easily. And in order to be completely comfortable with her new place in Washington, the center- piece of her living room at home in Millbrook, New York, was also shipped to Columbia Heights. The long, irregular, richly finished walnut slab coffee table with a partly ragged edge, made by George Nakashima fifty years ago was her favorite possession.

Lydia had gone to an estate auction in Atlanta for the contents of a mansion owned by a member of the Candler family that had owned Coca Cola. She was accompanied by Jane Fonda who at the time was married to Ted Turner. Jane knew Nakashima's work and urged Lydia to keep bidding on the table. The piece was so beautifully crafted that it was actually a one-of-a- kind art composition that was also a practical piece of elegant furniture, and it was signed by the artist which made it even rarer. Lydia's last bid of $19,000 was accepted.

The district congressional offices were located in Poughkeepsie and Peekskill, New York at the ends of Westchester and Dutchess Counties. Lydia came back to her district every other weekend, and for special events such as college commencements and high school reunions. The district staff made appointments, arranged White House tours and passes to the Capital. The chief-of-staff at home was a long-time confident, a retired professor and best-selling writer known as Kavanagh whose relationship with Lydia had developed over thirty years. During the 1990s, Kavanagh was chairman of the undergraduate social work department at a college of the City University of New York. Lydia, recovering from her second divorce, and needing a job, was the department secretary. As an unusually beautiful and stylish woman, Lydia always attracted attention, and for two years she had been married to the Manhattan celebrity agent, talent manager and promoter Bobby Vann. They were regulars at Elaine's, the Carlisle, Roxy, and the

Limelight, at times in the company of Jackie Kennedy, Mick Jagger, Madonna, Jon and Dorothea Bon Jovi and Calvin Klein.

Bobby Vann died in a boating accident off Fire Island during the summer of 1990, two years after their divorce, leaving Lydia his villa in Akumal, Mexico. During the Thanksgiving holiday that year, Lydia invited Kavanagh to accompany her to Mexico to file the paper work that would establish her ownership of the property that overlooked the sea. Kavanagh, dumfounded by Lydia's suggestion because they had not spent any time together outside of their workplace, eagerly accepted her invitation. They spent three days and one night together, and after that didn't see each other for almost twenty five years.

CHAPTER 7

Knox College, February 8, 2023

The Hallmark Valentine card arrived two weeks early. It was delivered with Lydia's new address on the envelope even though all of her other mail arrived with yellow stickers forwarded by the Post Office. The card wasn't signed, but it contained the following note.

A meeting will be held at Knox College on February 8 at 1 pm. All previous procedures are to be observed. DESTROY THIS NOTE

This time there was no consideration of voting rules so the discussion putting forth names begun as soon as everyone was seated. Significantly Shaughnessy was not mentioned and no one brought up the fact that Steve Bannon apparently disappeared while traveling from Budapest to Krakow and possibly then to Prague. No one was certain about Bannon's travel arrangements, which he kept to himself in order to avoid interruptions. Whether or not Bannon decided to go underground for a while to escape the negative attention in the media or the decision was made for him was a cause for speculation.

Perhaps the fates of both men were on the minds of the six members of the panel as new names were put up for consideration.

Steve Mellor who had been brought to prominence in Washington by Senator Jeff Sessions of Alabama was the first to be examined. Previously Mellor had worked for Republican Congresswoman Michele Bachmann considered in Washington to be the stupidest member of congress in her time, and a founder of the defunct Tea Party. Sessions introduced Mellor to Trump who quickly identified with Mellor's anti-immigrant, anti-Hispanic, anti-black and anti-Chinese rhetoric. Upon learning that Osama Bin Laden was considered a hero by Mellor, Trump brought him into the White House inner circle. Mellor's family were Jewish immigrants who escaped from the pogroms in Belarus a part the Russian Empire in 1903 and fled to America.

Somehow Mellor became an extremist, a right wing hater of almost everyone except people in power after reading a book by Wilson DePeters of the ARA. Now at the Knox College meeting, the Professor began the indictment against Mellor, especially Mellor's plan, put in motion in 2018, to separate migrant children from their families and hold them in cages reminding many of the German death camps that overflowed with tragic humanity in the 1940s. This attack on innocent families, especially children, was applauded by Trump's white Christian evangelical infused base of supporters that very much wanted to hurt these people who had dared to try to come to America seeking refuge.

Mellor's wife, Katy Rose an inhumane, anti-social psychopath who had dismissed the tragedy of family separation while speaking for the Trump administration was also considered by the Knox group.

The Advocate speaking up for the first time reminded the members that they were not to seek revenge for past crimes, but they must indict for creating current threats to democracy and the Constitution. By using these terms, Lydia supposed that the Advocate was a lawyer, and with that knowledge she was sure of her identity. In a legal fashion, the Advocate laid out a case against Steve Mellor who had become the darling of most of the nation's hate groups. He appeared on stages with brown military uniformed goons wearing red arm bands with a lightning bolt in a white circle. Mellor was thin to the point of being gaunt. He appeared to current historians to fit comfortably into the Nazi mold of *Gruppenfuhers* Hitler's main lieutenants, especially Adolf Eichmann the designer of what resulted in the Holocaust. Eichmann was the architect of "The final solution to the Jewish question."

Mellor certainly had been the designer of Trump's final solution for the southern border's immigrant crisis. The Advocate warned that currently Mellor was proposing a version of eugenics a phony science popular in the 1930s that sought to control America's black population, which was considered to be inferior. He had raised large sums of money from wealthy fascists that supported almost anything that claimed to stop the coloring of America.

Eugenics had become a passion of Hitler's in his quest to create a super race. It was because of its identification with the Nazis that the death knell for eugenics was finally sounded in the United States. The case for Mellor's elimination was detailed and complete as put forth by the Advocate so no other discussion was introduced. Lydia who had planned to bring up additional material condemning Mellor changed her mind and simply asked for a vote. The result was five yes and a single no by the Scientist.

As the discussions continued, peoples' names were tossed about and the fortunate ones were excluded. Lydia wondered if a similar process had taken place in 2019 in regard to Jeffrey Epstein, the convicted pedophile and sex trafficker. The re-opened investigation concerning Epstein's sexual abuse of young girls also netted other well-known individuals. Most prominently mentioned was Ghislaine Maxwell, daughter of British media tycoon Robert Maxwell, and darling of the Euro-trash set. She was accused of being Epstein's "pimp." Ghislaine had introduced England's Prince Andrew to Epstein and a long friendship centered on sex with underage girls ensued. The most egregious suspected involvement in Epstein's circle of pedophilia was retired Harvard Law professor Alan Dershowitz, a self-appointed moralist and defender of Donald Trump. Trump was another Epstein friend and once said that he and the pedophile had similar interests in beautiful young women. Who, Lydia wondered, had made the decision to kill Epstein before he identified to authorities more of the many prominent people he had involved sexually with underage girls?

Once again, the ugly head of Attorney General Bill Barr appeared. He claimed to be "appalled" by the suspected suicide of Epstein while in federal custody. Barr himself had a long relationship with Epstein since Barr's father Donald hired the unqualified Epstein in 1976. At the time Epstein was a young college dropout, but was hired to teach mathematics at Dalton, one of the most prestigious private schools in the nation. Perhaps headmaster Donald Barr knew of Epstein's ability to recruit pre-teen girls for sex with older men.

While in federal custody in New York City during August of 2019, Epstein was found dead in his cell. He had hung himself the story said, but how did it happen as Epstein was watched by TV cameras and guards. Suddenly the systems failed and he died. Was Epstein killed by an earlier version of the Knox group? A different purpose group devoted to the protection of prominent people like Dershowitz and Trump from prosecution and ruin rather than protecting democracy.

About a month after the Knox College meeting, Mellor, after leaving a private jet, was being transported, in order to avoid the surface traffic, by helicopter from Teterboro Airport in New Jersey to lower Manhattan. He was to speak at a Holocaust denier's demonstration in front of the Museum of Jewish Heritage at the Battery. As the unmarked Bell Cobra approached the building with the several hundred demonstrators kept across the street by police, a hatch on the craft's side away from the pilot opened and a man fell two hundred feet landing in the building's plaza. Before the body was even identified, Lydia realized that it was Steve Mellor who lay smashed and bloody on the stone surface by the place that implored everyone to never forget the murderous times in Europe when more than six million Jews, Catholic priests and nuns, Gypsies, homosexuals, the disabled, and others deemed to be undesirable were systematically killed by the "perfect" German super race.

Lydia was dreaming about the people the Knox group had considered and some that had been condemned. She awoke suddenly, perspired and confused. The face of a woman she didn't know had filled her sub-conscious thoughts. The woman's head was tipped back as if she was gasping for air and seeking relief from her precarious position. Lydia got out of bed. It was 6 am, and she went to her new kitchen. She drew a glass of cold water from the spout on the door of the stainless-steel refrigerator and drank it all down. Feeling better, she returned to her and bedroom picked up the iPhone on the night table. An email story from *The New York Times* proclaimed, "Controversial Evangelist Drowned in Own Pool."

The evangelist, Constance Driscoll-Bush was discovered last night around 11 pm drowned in the in-ground pool of her 4970 square foot home on Belle Meade Lane in the most expensive section of Memphis, Tennessee. A photo of Driscoll-Bush preaching in her Church of the Constant Adoration accompanied the article. Lydia almost fainting dropped on her bed. In the photo, the evangelist's head was back as if seeking divine guidance. However her face showing pain was the same image from Lydia's dream experienced only minutes ago.

Constance Driscoll-Bush had been marked for death by the Knox group because she was assembling an armed force estimated to have a membership of over twenty thousand men and women. Called, *The Army of the Heartland,* it was composed of weekend warriors who at first were engaged in playing soldier at the thousand acre camp grounds owned by Driscoll-Bush in the Smokey Mountains of Tennessee.

However, due to the immediate financial success of the make believe army, the evangelist hired former Army and Marines drill instructors and created a basic training curriculum that went along with her passionate preaching of the Gospel of Defense. She welded followers into an intimidating force armed with assault weapons that showed up at public events. Legal in Tennessee, where gun ownership was a sacred right, Driscoll-Bush's army had become a threatening force to the point that people stayed away from polling places, high school athletic events and holiday parades fearing confutation with the self-important, illegitimate, fraudulent soldiers.

Driscoll-Bush had become a concern to members of the Knox group because she was poised to bring her "army" to several other places in states of the South and Southwest and establish new training camps for new armies. Scores of people were willing to pay the $2 thousand annual dues to get to parade in military formulation, learn infantry tactics from professionals and fire all sorts of weaponry. And, the most attractive part was the chance to appear in public places armed and in uniform in order to make the point that America was not going to be turned over to immigrants even those who had been brought here against their will almost four hundred years before. Driscoll-Bush's sermons were fiery orations demanding that white Americans defend themselves against the encroaching tide of humanity, who were only seeking to survive the cruelty that their life had dealt them.

Driscoll-Bush's personal fortune quickly grew, she had created her army only five years ago. She bought radio stations on which her brand of poison would be heard twenty-four hours a day. Featuring the worst of the lying radio hucksters, Alex Jones, Laura Ingraham, Ann Coulter and Rush Limbaugh, the radio stations catered to the rural listeners who wanted to blame anyone except themselves for their life's failures and lack of future. The people who never had aspirations or dreams found their solace in too much alcohol, opioids and radio trash telling them that nothing about their miserable lives was their fault.

CHAPTER 8

Columbia Heights, Washington, DC

Restaurants were lined up along 11th Street NW in Columbia Heights two streets from Lydia's townhouse. Several featured Asian cuisines that served odd dishes that Lydia didn't understand and certainly didn't want to eat. Bad Saint, a Filipino restaurant was the most popular and actually had a national reputation. Dinner reservations were difficult to achieve there even for a member of congress, which was all right with Lydia since the menu items included tuna jaw and pigs ears. She wasn't a foodie because her daily intake of food didn't reach the suggested 2000 calories recommended for good health. By rarely finishing any meal, Lydia maintained her willowy slender figure and her body weight had not changed since graduating college thirty five years ago. Tonight she was meeting the occupant of the second floor apartment in her townhouse. Jenny Saito was the junior senator from Hawaii, a second term Democrat just a few years older than Lydia. She traveled back to Honolulu only about once a month during the times congress was in session. Her husband taught history at the University of Hawaii so the Senator lived by herself in the District. It was good fortune for both Lydia and Jenny that they had found each other when the Senator was looking for a new Washington address.

They dined together at least once a week either at Red Rocks where thin individual margarita pizza was served or at Letena an

Ethiopian restaurant where Lydia enjoyed the *kik wot,* yellow split peas simmered in a spicy sauce or *yemisir wot,* red lentils sautéed and scooped up with *injera* the flat bread served at every meal. The Senator usually ordered a version of steamed fish made with exotic herbs, lots of spices and unusual vegetables. Lydia avoided eating fish at Letena because tilapia was listed on the menu, which is a farm raised warm water variety that some people consider suspicious because of crowded fish breeding tank conditions around the world.

Lydia and the Senator shared gossip, Washington's main product, and confided in each other regarding their party's planned legislation, committee work and complained about the slow pace of restoring the government to at least its level of functioning prior to the great debacle of the Trump years.

Tonight the Senator was unhappy. One of her colleagues from across the aisle, the closeted Senator from South Carolina had been killed in a hit and run accident the night before. "I don't know how that could have happened," she exclaimed. "We never agreed on anything, but he was always pleasant to me, and was welcoming when I was first elected. I have a feeling it wasn't an accident. I don't know why, but there have been several murders recently including the possibility of the majority leader's death not being a suicide. The FBI has been quiet about it even though two of its agents were in the leader's office at the time. None of the deaths have been explained and no one has been apprehended to my knowledge." Lydia just listened. She knew for a fact that Senator from South Carolina had not been selected as a target of the Knox group. His name hadn't been introduced, ever, so she could honestly wonder along with Jenny Saito about the circumstances of the incident. However, he had been Trump's most stalwart supporter, and there still are people who hated anyone who blindly supported Trump, the most corrupt and incompetent elected official in American history.

Jenny Saito was born in Japan. Her parents moved to Hawaii when she was a little girl and they all became naturalized citizens.

"Who would have thought that a Japanese-American woman could ever be elected to the United States Senate?" she asked rhetorically. Saito had been one of the most outspoken critics of Trump, calling him in televised interviews, "a grifter and a criminal." She knew her way around Washington even before her election to the Senate as she had graduated from the Georgetown University Law Center, a cauldron of aspiring politicians. She enjoyed Lydia's friendship especially once she learned that her friend had a long career in television in Atlanta, was connected to Ted Turner and closely associated with the Obamas.

Later that night as Lydia tried to sleep, she thought about the potential reaction to the Knox group's narrow decision to spare the congresswoman from Wyoming. When her name was brought up the group became quiet and one by one each member related his or her negative opinion. She was considered in some circles the most dangerous elected official in the country because of her extreme right wing personal agenda that attracted like-minded deranged followers. It's possible that some of the Knox group were also expressing their hatred for her father who had been considered America's most powerful vice president due to serving with America's weakest president George W. Bush, also considered the dumbest until Trump, who abrogated his duties to the vice president.

The tragedy of Iraq, the nation's longest war, was created and sold to the congress by the vice president in order to enrich himself and his friends especially through his company Halliburton and its spinoff KBR, Inc. And during the Iraq War a new money making phenomenon found its way to the battlefield. A company known as Blackwater supplied thousands of "contractors" to perform security services in Iraq that had traditionally been carried out by United States service personnel under the typical chain of military command and the Uniform Code of Military Justice. Basically Blackwater supplied mercenaries paid on average $6000 a week tax free by Eric Prince the company's owner.

Prince was paid three times as much by the government for each man in the field. After numerous civilian killings carried out by Blackwater that attracted loud criticism from the media, the public questioned why mercenaries were hired by the government in the first place. Prince then wrote a syrupy book about his life as a misunderstood rich boy just doing his duty. Even worse than Prince was his sister Betsy DeVos, Trump's Secretary of Education who was a shill for the for-profit education field a billion dollar system of costly mostly mediocre and worse colleges and trade schools with only the few exceptions where students learned automotive and mechanical technology.

The Wyoming congresswoman escaped the Knox group's attention because Lydia and the Scientist voted against her being sanctioned. The reason she was brought to the group's attention was in part her father's fault.

CHAPTER 9

Dutchess County, NY

New York's 18th Congressional District follows the eastern Hudson Valley from upper Westchester to Dutchess County. The district's socio-economic overview ranges from lower middle to extremely wealthy with mostly middle class enclaves. There isn't much industry and retail and service businesses make up the majority of the commerce found in the commuter towns that send their residents to Manhattan every week day.

Lydia's district office in Westchester was located in Peekskill an old city on a bay of the Hudson River. By taking the Metro North Railroad, Manhattan can be reached in seventy minutes, which helped to make Peekskill an affordable bedroom community for New York City.

The office was staffed by one full-timer and several part-timers, as well as volunteers when events and mailings needed additional hands. Both offices, Peekskill and the one in Poughkeepsie, were supervised by Lydia's friend, confident and long ago lover Dr. Kavanagh. Kavanagh had retired after a career as professor of social work at the City University of New York. He had moved from an apartment in the Kips Bay section of Manhattan near NYU Medical Center to Peekskill. Living in Manhattan had become too expensive to maintain with his limited income. Kavanagh received Social Security and the annual required distribution of his 401 (K) held by TIAA the private national pension system for college and university faculty members. Royalties from Kavanagh's bestselling book, *The God Myth,* which normally were paid to him, were tied up in litigation with the publisher because Kavanagh had refused to promote the book on television or at in-person book signings.

He left the city when his apartment lease was up for renewal with a large increase in the rent, and bought a two bedroom with two bath condominium in the Chapel Hill complex in Peekskill. The property had housed the St. Florence Catholic Convent for about a hundred years. Kavanagh's two grown children and two grandchildren lived in lower Westchester so he was no further away from them than when he lived in Manhattan.

Kavanagh had purchased his flat on a hill overlooking a bay in the spring of 2019 for $330,000. His monthly mortgage payment at 4.12% interest was $1160. Adding taxes, association fee and homeowner's insurance brought his monthly expense to $1798, significantly less than a third of the cost of staying in his rented Manhattan apartment. The tax advantage created by home owner-ship had been wiped away by Trump and the Republicans in 2018 when they passed, without a single hearing, a new tax law penal-izing homeowners in the Northeast and California where property values and real estate taxes are the highest.

On a Saturday in September, Kavanagh was having lunch on Division Street, Peekskill's center for restaurants and shopping. Rueben's Mexican Café was a favorite and it was busy. A young woman approached his table offering a brochure describing the Democrat's candidate for congress in the upcoming election. Kavanagh accepted the paper folder to be polite and put it aside to concentrate on the chicken fajita and bottle of Corona with a lime wedge stuck in its top that had been served to him.

Later while waiting for his credit card to be processed, Kavanagh idly picked up the brochure left on his table. He was startled to learn that the candidate running for congress as a Democrat was indeed Lydia Merriman. Lydia and Kavanagh had a long history together, over thirty years, however, during most of that time they neither saw nor heard from each other.

Lydia was the woman always in his thoughts since the time they spent a few days together in Mexico in 1990, after which Lydia disappeared from his life. She showed up in dreams and fantasies, and when his mind wasn't crowded with other thoughts, Lydia's face would appear with a smile that Kavanagh found charming and seductive and irresistible to him. He had been in love with her since their first impromptu dinner date in Greenwich Village's Minetta Tavern over three decades ago. The next day Kavanagh called the number on the campaign brochure and told the woman answering the phone that he wanted to become a volunteer supporting Lydia's campaign. He asked to speak with the candidate, saying he was an old friend, but Lydia was out campaigning. Two hours later she called back.

Kavanagh spent most days that fall campaigning for Lydia. Sometimes she would ask him to accompany her to evening events where she spoke to community groups, associations or debated her Republican opponent. The opponent, a Wall Streeter ready to retire from the world of finance especially after losing most of his fortune investing in Bitcoin, actually resided in Manhattan, but owned a weekend home in Dutchess County. Last year, he and his wife changed their voting registration to Rhinebeck in the 18th congressional district.

However, when Lydia asked Kavanagh to accompany her to Setoncliff University near Poughkeepsie to appear at a rally sponsored by the campus chapter of Young Democrats, he refused claiming another appointment. Lydia thought it was odd because Kavanagh had been a visiting scholar at the university. When she met the university's president, Sister Mary Lucy, an attractive stylishly dressed woman, Lydia correctly suspected that something may have happened between Kavanagh and her.

CHAPTER 10

Knox College, May 4, 2023

A t the next meeting of the Knox group, names of individuals were brought up and discarded. The Philanthropist suggested Ivanka Trump and her husband Jared Kushner. They weren't seriously considered for the group's attention, but their mere presence in print and on television angered the majority of Americans. The Professor spoke up. "I don't believe they're a threat as the pretenders to the throne used to be in Europe. They're just annoying."

The Advocate, whose comments sometimes revealed knowledge of pending actions by federal prosecutors said, "I believe the happy couple received target letters from the Justice Department, and a RICO investigation of their predicate offences has begun." Lydia asked for an explanation. "I understand," the Advocate responded, "money laundering, wire and mail fraud, and extortion are the charges against them." The news cheered up all six sitting around the table. Continuing, the Advocate explained that if indicted, tried and found guilty, the Trump family members would forfeit everything they owned that was acquired through money gained illegally, everything.

"That means Jared will lose his little boy suits that make him look like Pee Wee Herman," ventured the Hippie. I still believe the Trumps, all of them, should be treated the same way the Bolsheviks dealt with the Tsar and his family in 1916. They removed the stain of royalty forever. Of course that was the only instance the Bolsheviks did anything right."

The group returned to the reason they were in rural Illinois at a secret meeting. They had to protect America from ever allowing a tyrannical authoritarian to again come close to threatening the very existence of the Constitution. And they intended to hobble the Republican Party for many years to come. With that mission in mind, they introduced a cascade of names. Eugene Meyer and Lawrence Leo of The Federalist Society, which has moved the nation's court system to the extreme right since George H.W. Bush was slipped into the presidency with the help of consultant Lee Atwater. Atwater employed unscrupulous and underhanded methods in Bush's behalf to eliminate popular Democratic contenders, especially Gary Hart, from consideration. Joel Osteen and Jerry Falwell, Jr. representing the pouting white evangelists, who spread hate and embraced totalitarian leaning politicians, were carefully examined as was Sarah Palin, whose brainless head was popping up on the extreme right again.

The Philanthropist brought up the slippery ministers Tony Perkins and Ralph Reed, two of the greatest hucksters selling their evangelism and family values while stealing with both hands. They were cheating everyone then ducking behind the white sheet of religion while waving the American flag, all while having a widening influence on enough people to be dangerous. Also it was rumored that Sarah Huckabee Sanders, known as "The Pig" was planning to run for the Senate from Arkansas. Was she a real threat? Sanders, a lying extreme right evangelical exactly like her father could be the harbinger of the old prediction, "When fascism comes to America it will be carrying a cross and wrapped in a flag."

The members debated the issues connected with each name. Even an Associate Justice of the Supreme Court, who had never rendered an opinion, was mentioned. His removal would open up a place for the appointment of a sorely needed liberal justice.

More names were introduced including Roger Stone, William Barr and the Kardashians, all of them. Some members laughed at that, but Lydia didn't. Some suggested names were rejected, and some were not.

That night leaving Galesburg and while driving to the London House, an elegant Hilton hotel in Chicago, Lydia felt as if she was becoming sick with flu or another illness that cause joint and body pain. She had hurried from the Knox group's meeting and drove away from the campus at a high speed. Lydia wanted to distance herself from the decisions made that day. She drove for three hours without thinking about anything except the road and getting far away from Galesburg.

There was a feeling of relief or escape as she approached Chicago. An hour before, Lydia had pulled off the highway and called the historic London House to reserve a suite with a view of the Chicago River. It was an image she always enjoyed. She hadn't eaten anything since breakfast which had consisted of coffee and a cranberry scone in a Starbucks. After checking in, room service delivered a chicken pot pie, Caesar salad, a small box of butter cookies and a half bottle of French Pinot Gris. The pot pie was tasty and Lydia finished its contents leaving the pie crust. She felt better and ate most of the salad, three cookies and drank all the wine.

By morning, Lydia decided to stay another night in Chicago. She informed the front desk that she would not be checking out as planned. The London House had been created within the walls of an historic landmark, the London Guarantee & Accident Building, opened in 1923 from the designs of noted Chicago architect Alfred Alschaler. Lydia paid the rate for federal employees for her suite, $296 plus tax, and $79 per day to park her rented car which she should have returned the day before. Lydia knew she had to answer the list of calls and texts on her iPhone.

Grace Ellen had called nine times, and sent more than a dozen texts. Kavanagh called four times. Lydia tapped Grace Ellen's number and the chief of staff answered immediately. "Where are you," Grace Ellen exclaimed in a nervous voice. "Are you all right? No one has heard from you."

"It's been two days. I'm in Chicago staying at the London House hotel. Why are you so upset?

"Because," Grace Ellen began as if talking to a child who didn't come back from recess, "Members of Congress don't disappear. They let someone know where they are at all times. I can't reach Kavanagh either. Is he with you?"

"No, of course he's not with me. Why would you ask me that?"

"I'm sorry, I'm sorry. Everyone has been looking for you. AOC herself has been here twice," Grace Ellen said referring to Alexandria Ocasio-Cortez the controversial congresswoman from New York's 14th Congressional District in the Bronx and Queens. "She wants to speak with you privately anywhere you say, not in Chicago."

"OK, ask AOC if she would rather talk in either office or meet for lunch at, let me think, Pembroke in the Dupont Circle Hotel any day we're both free. If she wants to have lunch, call the Pembroke, speak to David, and he'll save the corner booth by the bar for us at 1 o'clock. Now I'm going to my spa day. Facial, Swedish massage, pedicure. I want to feel pretty."

Grace Ellen's reaction was swift. "Oh come on, you're gorgeous. The last thing you need is more beauty. When will you be back? I have to answer the growing pile of requests for your presence."

"I'm going to New York from here and will see you Monday morning. And, I'm presenting you with a day at Massage Envy to calm you down a little bit. I won't pick up calls for the rest of the day."

CHAPTER 11

Rayburn Office Building, Washington, DC

R eturning to Washington on Monday, Lydia was immersed into a busy time on the Hill. Grace Ellen, Lydia's chief of staff had made the case for adding two new staff people to handle the work related to the committees Lydia sat on, but Lydia was reluctant to engage people quickly unless she knew their work habits and interpersonal skills. The chief seemed to spend days, nights, and weekends in the office playing catch up, and appeared on the verge of collapsing.

Lydia was deeply involved with the Congressional Black Caucus, and made appearances around the country in support of minority group candidates for state legislatures. She and the Caucus believed change must begin on the state level in order to overcome the decades of the Republican gerrymandering of congressional districts as carried out by state governments. The ultra-conservative majority of the Supreme Court found it to be just fine to disadvantage untold numbers of voters, especially black voters, and to blatantly benefit Republican politicians. Lydia was also called on to co-sponsor bills that dealt with healthcare, environmental protection, women's issues, and reclaiming public lands that had been allowed to be sold off during the darkest days of the Trump administration. She and her lawyer staffers carefully considered the proposals searching for any undesirable additions and other issues that could cause trouble once the bill was introduced.

Lydia had returned from the morning meeting of the Education and Labor Committee. The members were taking up the issue of free college tuition for everyone. Clearly it was a proposal that was well meaning, but controversial and she was trying to develop her own policy on the issue. The plan had been hanging around Washington since Bernie Sanders made it the center piece of his annoying bid for the presidency again in 2020.

Bernie kept sputtering and pushing his plan to make every state university and community college tuition free. Perhaps he didn't know that the United States government thankfully didn't control higher education except for the service academies. Perhaps Bernie had been advised on college control by his wife the former president of Burlington College. Jane O'Meara Sanders had bankrupted the small college in Vermont and caused financial scandal and chaos leaving students to scramble for admission to other places. Jane was investigated by the Justice Department for her role in the purchase of a two-million-dollar property to build her dream college while the student enrollment was less than two hundred.

There had been accusations of interference by Bernie in the investigation of financial improprieties during the foolish and inappropriate attempted expansion of the tiny college. The questionable real estate transaction took place during the beginning of the nation's lowest college student enrollment in a half century. Jane had wedeled $200,000 in severance pay from the struggling college while the minimum wage cafeteria workers went unpaid.

Lydia was about to begin a scheduled meeting with the Hudson River Riverkeeper and the vocal supporters of a cleaner river. The river's condition had been a major issue since folk singer Pete Seeger, using the sloop *Clearwater* as a center piece, began the annual event in 1966 known as the Great Hudson River Revival to call attention to the chemicals found in the majestic river. The pollution stemmed from dumping massive amount of PCBs up-river by the GE Corporation decades ago.

The river became a Super Fund project, and clean-up had been slow, but effective. However, recently environmental groups had made demands calling for action against the companies contracted to do the federally financed cleanup, claiming incompetence and the resulting shoddy work product in their beloved river.

Lydia was going through the stack of phone messages from staff of the committee chairs, the speaker's office and constituents before the River Keeper's meeting. The television monitors in her outer office were tuned all day to CNN, MSNBC and C-Span with the sound turned off. Suddenly Lydia heard a cry from the office staff. "Oh my god, somebody killed that son of a bitch."

There was scrambling and loud comments, and as Lydia quickly walked to the other room she looked up at the CNN monitor and saw an earnest young woman reporting from the street in the Sandy Hook neighborhood of Newtown, Connecticut. It took her a moment to realize that the camera was trained on a section of a wrought iron fence with sharp twisted spikes on top that ran along the side property of the 150-year-old St. John's Episcopal Church that had closed in 2018 due to the congregation's aging and leaving the area.

The reporter explained that less than an hour ago nearby, similar spikes had impaled the body of hate-radio personality Alex Jones. Both CNN and MSNBC refused to show the image of Jones spread on the fence face down with the spikes penetrating his body. A photo had been taken by a passing driver on his way to the train station. After calling 911, the driver couldn't resist taking a picture with his phone. Later, when he learned that the victim was Alex Jones, who brought even more heartbreak to a community devastated by the murder of twenty of its children, the image was sent to the Associated Press and *The New York Times*.

CHAPTER 12

Millbrook, NY May 7, 2023

In order to catch the daily 8 am non-stop Delta flight from O'Hare to Stewart Airport in Newburgh, NY, Lydia awoke at 5:30 to be ready for the hotel's 6:30 airport shuttle. She had returned the rented car through the Hertz desk in the lobby the day before. The hour and twenty minute flight landed on time at the former Air Force base now operated by the Port Authority as a civilian airport serving the counties between Poughkeepsie and Albany.

She was met by a driver for the car service she always used when going to or coming from the airport. The middle age man took off his Mets cap and greeted Lydia respectfully. He took hold of the carry on and led her to a black SUV with discrete signage. The driver opened a rear door and informed Lydia that bottles of cold water were in the small cooler next to her on the seat. Lydia was impressed with the manner that a white man, a rural area resident treated her, a client of course, but a black woman client. Perhaps as the song said so long ago, "The times they are a-changin." Or was it the 25% tip she had authorized to be added to all charges she incurred with the car service?

The driver left Lydia at her district office in the center of Poughkeepsie on a block with three-and-four-story buildings that had housed department stores, insurance companies and clothing stores, but now were mostly empty. By selecting a space on a one of the city's quiet central streets, Lydia believed she was helping in a small way to energize the business district that was made up of some new and a few old restaurants, health and beauty products shops, nail salons and lawyer's offices.

She was greeted enthusiastically by the district staff, and spoke to each of them to gain feedback as to what was happening in her district over the last two weeks. Lydia was especially interested in the responses to the several hundred weekly email messages the office received from constituents and the nature of the replies. Kavanagh had recruited one of his former graduate students to carefully handle email responses exclusively. Was Lydia being informed of situations that had potential to become serious problems, she always wanted to know.

Her schedule that day included meetings with the County Executive, a fellow Democrat and a supporter, another meeting with Poughkeepsie's deputy mayor, a Republican ready to criticize if Lydia didn't deliver a desired federal program, whether or not the city was eligible. Lunch with the leadership of the Board of Realtors at the Grand Hotel near the Hudson River was at 1 pm. And finally a presentation at three o'clock at the Vassar-Warner Home established in 1871 as a place for adults who were unable to live alone any longer. It offered a dignified late life plan that possibly was the first "assisted living" facility in the nation. After spending time with individual residents, mostly women who were charmed with Lydia's genuine friendliness and concern, she said goodbye promising to return.

The same black SUV waited in the circular driveway, and as Lydia approached the same driver quickly greeted her tipping his hat and opening a rear door for her. The drive to Millbrook and her home took about twenty minutes and Lydia was relieved to see her house where she anticipated turning off her phone and lounging and sleeping until the next day.

She had moved to Millbrook from Atlanta in 2015. The hamlet was an exclusive enclave with only about 1,200 residents. Lydia's nearest neighbor was the actor Liam Neeson, whom she had known from her days at Turner television. Neeson suggested that Lydia consider living in Millbrook when she was planning to return to New York, and informed her when a classic home was on the market. She committed to purchase the house after touring it on-line and then took a quick flight from Atlanta to sign the contract.

Awakening the next morning at 7 o'clock, Lydia instinctively reached for her phone and read the headlines. A coal baron from West Virginia, a buddy of Trump, accused of so many crimes against the environment and worker's safety, but never convicted, had died in a hospital prior to having routine heart surgery for a single bypass. The death was a shocking surprise to the family and doctors, but not to Lydia since the coal baron had been marked for attention at the first meeting of the Knox group. Trying to not think about who would be the next headline, Lydia took a long shower then a steam shower, dressed casually and made a pot of French roast coffee in anticipation of her meeting with Kavanagh at 10 o'clock.

On the weekends she was home in the district, Lydia and Kavanagh met in Millbrook for an hour or two or until Lydia was to appear at some political, social or educational function accompanied by Kavanagh. Kavanagh lived about a forty minute drive south in Peekskill. He had found a good bagel bakery there, and always brought two poppy seed bagels, well done, two plain bagels and a container of vegetable cream cheese. Even though Lydia would nibble on a half of the plain bagel with a hint of cheese, and Kavanagh would have one poppy seed bagel covered with the spread, he continued to purchase four bagels as he believed that ordering only two would make him appear needy.

He arrived exactly at 10, ringing the doorbell. They embraced quickly, smiled at each other, and Kavanagh followed Lydia to the elegantly equipped kitchen, installed when she purchased the white clapboard, with pale blue shutters, century old colonial house. At the granite surface table, Kavanagh unpacked his briefcase. Lap top, loose leaf file, note pad, and iPhone were ready for use. He brought Lydia up to date on all of the issues that had come to his attention lately and glancing at the notepad he reminded Lydia of the two commencement appearances she had promised to make in two weeks. At one, Setoncliff University, Lydia was to receive an honorary doctor of humanities degree. At Dutchess Community College, she'll deliver the commencement address. "Tammy," referring to a lawyer on the Washington staff, "is writing my talk for Dutchess and I'll have her send it to you for your reaction." Honorary degree recipients usually don't offer remarks so no prep was necessary for the Setoncliff event. Then she ominously asked, "Kavanagh, will you come with me to Setoncliff, or don't you want to run into the pretty nun?"

Kavanagh, surprised by the question simply said, "I'll come with you," and to himself he acknowledged there was some history between himself and the president of Setoncliff, Sister Mary Lucy. Referring to his notes again he said, "Look both Vassar and Marist College have invited you to commencements, symposia, convocations. You have to attend something on each campus. The Culinary Institute in Hyde Park has not invited you. Probably because they know you don't cook and this kitchen is only for show." He smiled, waiting for a defensive claim of cooking prowess. Lydia ignored him and pointed to the list on the notepad.

"OK, you had lunch with AOC. What's up?"

"She asked me to help her out as if we were old friends. I was surprised because we haven't really talked even though we both represent New York. And I discovered that she's not from the city. She grew up in Westchester in Yorktown Heights. Not that it matters, but it puts a different slant on her message."

Kavanagh said, "Yeah I knew that, but she's a made a splash. I think she's smart. What does she want you to do?" He had re-evaluated AOC after her unwise support of Bernie Sanders in 2020, but kept that opinion to himself.

Lydia took a breath, "AOC asked me to campaign in Detroit with Rashida Tlaib because she has a strong challenger in the primary. Rashida's district has 40% black voters and they don't feel she's representing their interests only the interests of Palestinians in the Middle East. I told AOC I won't campaign for Rashida as her black prop."

"What was her reaction?"

"She was OK. I imagine she was fulfilling a promise she made to Rashida to ask me for help. And when I said, no, that was the end of it." Lydia heated up both cups of coffee. "She had another question. Next year Kirsten's Gillibrand's senate seat is up. She has to stand for re-election. AOC believes that her run for the presidency highlighted just how ordinary Kirsten is. It was a big mistake. Actually Kirsten's only real accomplishment was getting Al Franken to resign."

Kavanagh interrupted by saying, "I never liked Al Franken as an entertainer, but he was a hell of a Senator. Of course feeling up women during photo shoots is as stupid as can be, so Al had to go. What the hell was he thinking? Only Trump was allowed to molest women without any consequences for him."

"Anyway," Lydia continued, "AOC asked if I going to challenge Kristen in the senate primary. A strong down state candidate could drop Kristen from the ballot. The population just isn't there for her to win. Also, her history is pretty right leaning on immigration and was against gun control in order to appease the upstate voters. As AOC put it, another woman, a woman of color with experience in Washington will capture the city, Long Island, the counties just north of the city, which wins it. It's the time for women to greatly influence national politics as Nancy Pelosi has proven."

Kavanagh agreed. "She's right. It's brilliant. I thought something was up with her since she stopped leading the Squad." He was referring to representatives Ilhan Omar of Minnesota, Rashida Tlaib of Michigan, and Congresswoman Ayanna Pressley of Massachusetts. Speaker Nancy Pelosi in 2019 called the Squad "irrelevant" after they voted against the border bill because it didn't include everything Democrats wanted." She said, "These people have their public whatever and their Twitter world. But they didn't have any following. They're four people and that's how many votes they have." Kavanagh asked with some apprehension, "So Lydia how did you answer AOC's question."

"I assured her that I didn't have an interest in running for the senate. Although having to run for re-election every two years is a challenge to my strength and my sanity. I didn't ask her if she'll run, but I think she will. And, just think about this. FDR, JFK, AOC. That girl is bad-ass, and she got it go-in on," Lydia said and then laughed.

"You know," said Kavanagh, "I love it when you try to sound black."

"I'm black Kavanagh. In case you forgot," and then they both laughed. At noon they left the house and went to the Vassar Brothers Medical Center where Lydia spoke briefly at the hospital's children's fair. She mingled around through the health stations, games and food tables chatting and listening to anyone who wanted to talk with her. The people with questions were asked to put their concerns in an email and she promised to answer them.

Kavanagh stayed away because Lydia didn't like the appearance of a politician with handlers around her. In fact she drove them to the fair in her Jeep Cherokee. During her first campaign, Lydia traded her Cadillac coupe for the more democratic appearing Jeep vehicle. Kavanagh watched the crowd enjoy Lydia's presence. The years of appearing on television in Atlanta polished her already dynamic personality and great appearance. He sighed and thought, after his two marriages and some long love affairs, no other woman had meant so much to him as Lydia or was so desired. The fact that the same feelings were not shared by Lydia didn't interrupt his devotion to her.

When she left Atlanta after an admirable career, Lydia felt that her life was beginning again. The move back to New York, seven years ago, had been on her mind for a while hoping that her twenty three year old son JC would somehow become a larger part of her life again. JC resided in San Diego after serving in the Navy. Lydia offered to arrange a job for him in the office of her Democratic colleague in California's 50th Congressional District, but JC refused preferring to work on the sightseeing boats operating in the city's harbor.

Lydia had also grown weary of the politics of race seriously practiced by Republicans in all of the states below the old Mason-Dixon Line. Not that New York was immune from racial politics, but it wasn't a daily exercise. What had brought Lydia to New York from Atlanta in 2015 was a plan to devote her considerable talents to the promotion of a dormant social theory, known as epigenetics or the science of change.

In the 1970's, social scientists postulated that the slave experience produced trauma in individuals that lasted for five generations in black families. Epigenetics, it was theorized actually traced chromosome changes that affected activity and expression that resulted in corrupted life styles for a large percentage of the nation's black population. Recently the study of epigenetics as a predictor of cancer had put the theory into the main stream of scientific research.

Lydia reasoned that it was the time to encourage the research necessary to interrupt the chromosome damage by the slave experience so that future generations of black children wouldn't be affected by their ancestors. After raising $5 million, including her own $1 million donation, a lab for the study of epigenetics was established at the Columbia University School of Public Health. Lydia continued to raise funds for the project through a foundation established for that purpose, and remained the foundation's chairperson and energetic leader until she was elected to Congress.

She was aware of the wide range of opinions on the validity of epigenetics. Kavanagh, a social scientist, had prepared a comprehensive review of the field's literature for Lydia five years ago. He like many others sided with *nurture* rather than *nature* when attempting to explain behavior. He postulated that the dominant culture's treatment of black people, not only in the South, had worn down the will of so many to try to achieve. In her literature class at Queen's College, Lydia had read William Faulkner's *The*

Sound and the Fury and became angry by his characterization of the black people living in the American South in the 1920s, as child-like accessories to the white's they served.

Also, she resented Faulkner's demeaning references to blacks who in 1930, sixty five years after the passage of the Thirteenth Amendment still barely existed as free people. Having grown up in New York with parents who were educated professionals, Lydia didn't have much knowledge regarding the lives of black people in the South prior to the era of Martin Luther King. Her mother had grown up in Alabama, but refused to talk about her life there, saying it was just better to forget the painful times. Lydia had read the work of Malcom X, also *Soul on Ice and Tally's Corner,* which were primarily about the black people who lived in northern cities, and of course some of James Baldwin's essays and poetry, but Faulkner's long-ago southland haunted her.

Years later while paging through an old copy of the *Southern Review,* Lydia came across an article by William Faulkner written in 1933 and published by the magazine in 1972. It was the introduction to a new edition of *The Sound and the Fury.* It began, "Art is no part of Southern life. In the North it seems to be different. It is the hardest minor stone in Manhattan's foundation. It is part of the glitter and shabbiness of the streets. But in the South art, to become visible at all must become a ceremony, a spectacle; something between a gypsy encampment and a church bazaar. Perhaps this is because the South is old since dead. New York, whatever it may believe of itself is young since alive, but the South is dead, killed by the Civil War."

As Faulkner was re-examining life in the South, The Harlem Renaissance had been on-going since 1918. Harlem in New York City had become the nation's center of black (at the time Negro) life. Jazz had come to Harlem from New Orleans. Painters, poets, writers, actors, singers and dancers frequented the smoky clubs and performed at the Apollo Theater on 125th Street, Harlem's heart, while black life in the South had largely gone unchanged since the failure of Reconstruction after the Civil War, which established the "Black Codes" that once again stole the freedom of the former slaves.

Lydia, in time, forgave Faulkner, but not the old South. In order to keep the South in the Union, Abraham Lincoln had conducted the nation's bloodiest war. Generations later, southerners were still displaying the rebel flag, and erecting statues to Confederate Army generals. The war had been lost, but not forgotten, and the members of the black population that remained there were the victims of the Confederacy's defeat.

Lydia wasn't immune to racial discrimination. No black person in America was, but she was more fortunate than most. She used to say, "Anthropology was the most useless college major, which ensured that no job in the field would ever be available. Therefore, I will not be disappointed by not getting hired because of my race."

CHAPTER 13

Lydia's Family

Lydia Merriman had grown up in South Jamaica a section of Queens County in New York City. Many of South Jamaica's African-American residents were middle class home owners, and Lydia's parents were professionals who provided a stable family life for their only child. Her dad, Joseph, was a pharmacist, a graduate of the Brooklyn College of Pharmacy from the time when he and another man who commuted from Rutherford, New Jersey were the only black students in their class.

Joseph was descended from an enslaved black family that had traveled from Virginia to Vermont in 1859 along the route of the Underground Railroad. They were met and housed by Daniel Merriman an abolitionist when they reached Bennington in southern Vermont. Daniel Merriman was a Congregational minister, and a graduate of Williams College. Joseph's ancestors, as a tribute to Daniel, adopted the name Merriman as their own upon leaving Vermont for New York soon after emancipation following the end of the Civil War.

Melinda, Lydia's mother was a librarian at the Queens Library at South Jamaica located within walking distance from her home. Melinda had been born and grew up in a section of Tuscaloosa, Alabama until graduating from Druid High School, the city's secondary school for black students. She excelled in a strong academic program designed to encourage black students to follow a teaching career. However after studying American literature at Mills College in Fairfield, Alabama, Melinda decided she would follow her passion for books and become a librarian. Mills, a private historically black college, offered traditional liberal arts study with teaching that was equal to any other fine college or university in the nation. By excelling at Mills and graduating with honors, Melinda was offered a fellowship to study library science at Columbia University in New York City, which she put off for three years in order to teach in Central High School to save up some money for travel to New York and living expenses in graduate school.

Arriving in New York in 1962, Melinda who hadn't traveled outside of Alabama before, found not a city of light, but rather a city on the brink of darkness. New York City was a financial disaster. Manufacturing had been leaving the city along with thousands of jobs. Street crime had increased dramatically while police budgets were reduced. The famous subway system was unsafe and dirty. Graffiti was everywhere inside and outside of trains and on station walls with no attempt to stop the aggressive spray painters. There were abandoned blocks of buildings in Harlem, the lower East Side of Manhattan, the South Bronx and many parts of Brooklyn. Times Square was infamous as the home of sex for sale in movies, live peep shows, and in person.

The city had been in trouble for years and sometime later when Mayor Abe Beame asked the federal government for a loan to stave off bankruptcy. President Gerald Ford, who had succeeded Richard Nixon, was not known for his intellectualism or empathy for the residents of states located on either coast. He vowed to veto any bailout of New York City that Congress passed. A headline of the *Daily News*, the newspaper with the largest circulation in the city boldly said, *"Ford to City – Drop Dead."*

However, the Morningside Heights campus of Columbia University was still a green oasis with classical buildings. Melinda's graduate program was fully paid for and living expenses were minimal except for meals because an apartment in a kind of grim university owned building was also included. Library Science was a two year full time graduate program and Melinda could only afford to travel back to her family in Alabama during the Christmas break and for the summer. Melinda's mother had recently retired from a career in teaching. She had taught in Tuscaloosa's segregated schools for forty years.

Melinda arrived home full of stories about New York being wonderful and terrible at the

same time. The public libraries were almost cathedrals compared to libraries in Alabama. The city's main library with its stone lions on 5th Avenue actually housed seven floors of

stacks below ground. Off-Broadway theater tickets were cheaper than movies. Used bookstores surrounded the campus along with restaurants that served food from exotic places with menu prices students could afford. She wisely avoided parts of the city. Even Greenwich Village with its music scene was unsafe at night for a woman by herself especially since it was a twenty-five minute subway ride back to Columbia. However the nearby Thalia movie theater on 95th Street and Broadway offered foreign and art films in her neighborhood for a fifty cents admission charge in an area that was always busy and usually safe.

While she was back at home in Tuscaloosa, Melinda planned to pack up the rest of her clothing and bring all of her skirts, pants and sweaters to New York. She was dismayed to discover that her closet and chest of drawers were almost empty. "Mama," she called out. "Where's my clothing?"

"Oh, I brought it all to the church for the poor," her mother explained smiling with the knowledge that she performed a kind act.

Melinda frustrated exclaimed, "Mama, we are the poor."

Upon returning to New York to finish her studies, Melinda met and fell in love with Joseph Merriman, a registered pharmacist employed by Lenox Hill Hospital in Manhattan. They married and when Melinda began her career at the Queens Library branch in South Jamaica, they purchased a home nearby so she could walk to work. Lydia was born one year later.

After attending the neighborhood elementary school, Lydia was slated to attend a middle school and later Jamaica High School. The schools had rough reputations and Melinda began a search for a private school for her daughter. After asking the staff and patrons of her library, Melinda discovered the Kew-Forest School founded in 1918 primarily for residents of Kew Gardens and Forest Hills.

Times change and the wealthy exclusive enclaves once found in Queens have melded into neighboring communities. The Kew-Forest School however, remained one of New York City's most expensive prep schools. Lydia was accepted and began the fifth grade without the benefit of a scholarship. The school's directors were not interested in diversity at the time. That did change, but not until Lydia had graduated. Her time at Kew-Forest was well spent. Besides completing a successful academic program, Lydia excelled in volleyball and tennis, and made some lasting friendships.

Because of the high tuition her parents had paid for Lydia's eight years at Kew-Forest, she enrolled in Queens College, a highly regarded public New York City college with a low tuition cost for the city's residents. Besides, Lydia loved New York, and wanted to stay in the city maintaining the associations made during her prep school time. The college boasted of its preforming arts alumni that included Jerry Seinfeld, Paul Simon, Marvin Hamlish, Ray Romano, Joy Behar, Fran Drescher, and Carol King. Lydia, as a theater minor enjoyed being a part of the college's show business history.

Queens College in the 1980s appeared to be a suburban campus with an abundance of trees, lawns and interesting original buildings. Lydia could imagine she was away at school if she wanted to, but most of the time she was happy being in the city.

Lydia's college major of anthropology and the theater arts minor kept her busy. Upon graduation she took a job in one of the small theaters on West 42nd Street in Manhattan that had undergone a renovation and was now a trendy off-Broadway venue. Lydia wasn't on stage; she was in the box office. The theater's owner, Bobby Vann was a powerful talent agent and raconteur, and was well known by everyone in entertainment, politics and the media. Vann hired the beautiful young recent college graduate, paid her lots of attention, and brought her into the nightlife of Manhattan's Café Society.

Bobby also enjoyed surprising his wide circle of sophisticated friends, and he did just that by marrying Lydia since they hardly knew each other. Interracial marriages in the late 1980s were rare even in New York. They divorced two years later, but remained close friends. Vann deeded to Lydia the apartment he owned outright in the Schwab House on West End Avenue. And when her second marriage ended after only six months, Vann arranged a job for Lydia, through Mayor Ed Koch, at the new College of Arts & Technology where she worked in Kavanagh's department.

They worked together for over a year. Dr. Kavanagh, the social work department's chairman, was titular boss of the faculty, whose members usually ignored his directives like all other tenured professors in the nation's system of higher education. Lydia was the department's secretary, and one evening, for the first time, they found themselves together outside of the college and dining at the Minetta Tavern in Greenwich Village.

The historic restaurant was a short walk from their office. Lydia, surprising Kavanagh, had invited him to join her at the restaurant. He happily agreed since he would not have asked her out, and they shared a pleasant talkative evening. She surprised him once again at the evening's end by asking Kavanagh to accompany her over the Thanksgiving holiday to Akumal, Mexico to claim the ocean front villa left to Lydia by her recently deceased former first husband.

After their short time together in Mexico, Kavanagh fell hopelessly in love with Lydia. During their time in Akumal there was some intimacy, but clearly no commitment of any sort on Lydia's part. Kavanagh vainly tried to stay in contact with her once they returned to New York, but Lydia disappeared from his life and they didn't see one another again for almost twenty five years.

Lydia had left New York in 1990. She was recruited by Ted Turner, whom she met through Bobby Vann, to develop programming for Turner television stations in Atlanta, Charlotte, North Carolina, Columbia, South Carolina and New Orleans that were focused on black viewers. She understood what had to be done to make the stations relevant to the new black professionals who were relocating to southern cities.

Lydia and her team of producers, writers, directors and on-air people consisting of mostly Spelman College and Morehouse College graduates changed television programming for the viewers and attracted first-rate sponsorships. When Lydia left Atlanta after almost twenty- five years with Turner Broadcasting, she had amassed a personal fortune due to a stunning career, and generous stock options.

CHAPTER 14

Gramercy Tavern, New York City
July 11, 2023

Today, Kavanagh was lunching with Millicent his former second wife who was also his literary agent. Millicent had invited him to have a lunch talk and they occupied a booth at Danny Meyer's Gramercy Tavern on 20th Street in the Flatiron District. The famous restaurant had a new-colonial décor making it intimate, warm and welcoming with revised lunch and supper menus. Kavanagh was defending his five year old decision to ignore the publisher's constant requests to promote his formerly bestselling book, *The God Myth*. "For Christ sake Kavanagh," Millicent sounding frustrated said, "You're so fucking stubborn. It's no wonder we didn't stay together."

"No Millicent, we didn't stay married because you met Peter the jock and left me while I was in Ireland." He was referring to Peter Kelly, a former sports writer and currently a broadcaster on the YES network.

She smiled tolerantly and said, "Anyway, how are your children?"

"Nina is fine as always. She moved her practice to Bronxville close to Lawrence Hospital, which has greatly improved now that it's affiliated with Weill-Cornel Medical Center. I don't understand the mania of hospitals absorbing other hospitals."

Millicent commented, "It's the new merger-and-acquisition game. Health care has become highly profitable."

"Yeah, and as long as it's controlled by Wall Streeters we will never have healthcare for all in our fragile society."

"Kavanagh you're always the social worker trying to make life better for everyone."

"No, actually I consider myself a social psychologist trying to understand the pathology of those in the limited opportunity class who constantly work against their own interests." Kavanagh hesitated before going on. He was in lecture mode. "Do you remember the Trump rallies? Hundreds of blonde women wearing red hats. Probably living in trailer parks, under educated, in dead end jobs, but happy to help prevent the establishment of decent health insurance for themselves, or a higher federal minimum wage, childcare assistance or anything else to make their lives better. They actually believed that the Republicans were interested in their welfare because the party is against immigration."

"Okay Kavanagh, I get it. Now what's Greg doing?" Millicent was referring to Kavanagh's son who was highly educated and had drifted from one career to another. "I believe he liked me. Nina always seemed to be evaluating me."

"Nina's a doctor. It's what they do. The good news is Greg has found a direction in life. His superb education has paid off and after running his own SAT tutoring business for five years, he landed a job at Dobbs as their director of college prep. That's a big deal at the Masters School because all of the students and their parents expect them to attend prestigious colleges."

Millicent smiling said, "Well I'm happy for him. He was passionate about his interests, just like you."

"Greg's also passionate about someone now. He's dating a young woman, a teacher at Dobbs. She's lovely, smart and happens to be a black woman. I hope they marry."

Millicent said, "Good luck to them whatever they decide to do, just don't push."

Kavanagh, thoughtful and serious said, "I actually believe inter-marriage between the races will save America. It's the only hope we have." Millicent's look was quizzical as Kavanagh continued. "Racism is ingrained in our society. Slavery of course, the Civil War, the repudiation of Reconstruction leading to legislated seg-regation established racism as the norm." He hesitated to see if Millicent was still listening. She was. "Of course progress was made during the Obama years, but then Trump took it all apart and we had to start over."

Millicent absorbed the history and was smiling when she said, "Kavanagh, I'm sure you're correct, but now you must allow me to make some money for both of us by re-publishing your book with the new forward. That will stop the publisher's lawsuit and get the international edition going again. What about it?" At that point their lunch was served. Poached lobster for Kavanagh and Arctic Char salad for Millicent accompanied by a chilled bottle of Louie Latour Sauvignon Blanc listed on the wine list at $165.

Kavanagh had written a hundred page essay that Millicent wanted to use as the book's introduction. She believed that a new edition of *The God Myth* would introduce Kavanagh's work to an emerging generation of atheists, fallen-away Catholics and disaf-fected Jews. A newly-revised edition along with proper promotion could revitalize Kavanagh's flagging career. So after due consider-ation he agreed to allow Millicent to do whatever she had to do.

Millicent was happy. "That's good, but Kavanagh, can I depend on you to put in the time required for promoting your book? That means as many network and cable news interviews we can arrange. What's your time commitment to Lydia Merriman?"

"Like all congressional aides, I'm at her beck and call. I'll talk with her. I assume it will be okay."

Millicent smiling said, "Is Lydia more than your employer? I saw her on NBC recently and she's beautiful. How long have you known her?"

Kavanagh sighed, "A while, but I hadn't seen her for five years. And no, there's nothing but a working relationship. When

I learned Lydia was running for Congress in my district, I volunteered to work for her campaign, and when she was elected, I became her district director." There was a lot more to the story, but Kavanagh didn't share it with Millicent.

Late in October of 2015, Kavanagh and Lydia had spent two days together in Watch Hill, Rhode Island's Ocean House an historic hotel, established during the Gilded Age overlooking Block Island Sound. Failing to develop a romantic relationship with Lydia when she relocated to New York, and after a couple of lunches together as well as Lydia's admission that he was not needed in her life, Kavanagh had given up on ever hoping to see her again. Surprisingly he had received an email message from Lydia, who was visiting friends in Providence, Rhode Island, urging him to join her at the Ocean House because they should, in her words, be together after all. Kavanagh, surprised and elated, drove from Manhattan to meet up with the woman who had for a long time been the center of his thoughts and dreams.

Kavanagh arrived at the Ocean House ahead of Lydia and waited in the elegant lobby that had been completely rebuilt using the original plans for the building. As he waited, his thoughts centered on wondering and hoping that she would really be coming to meet him. When Lydia strolled through the hotel's main entrance, pulling a small overnight suitcase, he was over joyed, and when she came toward him arms wide, head high with a beautiful smile, Kavanagh was overwhelmed with emotions that had been building up for a long time.

After two rounds of sidecar cocktails served to them in the Bistro Bar, Lydia and Kavanagh relaxed and affectionate with each other, took the lobby elevator to their ocean-front suite on the hotel's third floor. Without any preliminary, Lydia closed the bedroom's drapes, they undressed and got into the king size bed from opposite sides. Their love-making was unhurried and natural to them as if they were lovers who happened to find themselves together.

The next day after a light breakfast, they walked along the beach south of the hotel. Kavanagh reminded Lydia that they had walked together on a beach in Mexico twenty five years ago almost to the day. Of course Lydia remembered, but she acted as if she didn't want to talk about that time, when she made the decision to leave New York and disappear from Kavanagh's life. Instead they talked about the views seen at Rhode Island's Napa Tree Beach, the magnificent crescent shaped shoreline. During their walk, which took most of the day. Kavanagh had stopped trying to anticipate Lydia's state of mind and instead he suggested they stop somewhere on Bay Street for a late lunch.

As they walked along Watch Hill's main street, Lydia's mood lifted, and she told Kavanagh that due to their long walk and sea air she actually was hungry. He was happy because he wondered how Lydia survived and looked so good while consuming so little food daily. They found the Olympia Tea Room a restaurant first opened in 1916. It was fortunate that the day was Monday as the Olympia was closed on Tuesdays. Once inside, they relaxed in an antique mahogany booth with a glass of white wine for Lydia and a Blue Moon draft beer for Kavanagh. The waitress tried to convince them to order the clam chowder, the best in New England she claimed, but neither one was interested. Instead Lydia selected the Old World Greek Salad, and Kavanagh the Flaked Haddock, a local fish, with spicy butter sauce.

While waiting for their food Kavanagh worried that Lydia had become vague. Was she re-thinking the decision to invite him to meet up with her? He wanted to talk about their next step together, but he was fearful of Lydia's reaction to anything that appeared to be heading toward a commitment. He didn't want to risk making the same mistake as when they were together in Mexico long ago. At the time, Kavanagh had believed he and Lydia had bonded after three days and nights together in a romantic tropical place. However when their plane landed at LaGuardia Airport in New York, Lydia picked her suitcase from the luggage carrousel and said goodbye to Kavanagh leaving his life for twenty five years.

Now at lunch in the Watch Hill restaurant, instead of a conversation about their being together, they talked about the Epigenetics project and Lydia's recent meeting at Massachusetts General Hospital that included a researcher from Harvard Medical School. She had traveled to Boston the week before, prior to coming to Rhode Island, to gather material for her upcoming meeting at Columbia University where the proposed research center would be established. She had been accompanied in Boston by the geneticist who will head the research team once the lab was established in New York.

Kavanagh was familiar with the field, but he wasn't convinced of its validity. However he listened rather than making his opinion known. Lydia's comments about her time in Boston demonstrated her mastery of the science, and her conviction that a destructive genetic link existed in black Americans that began as a result of slavery and has continued to the present. Lydia's excitement and enthusiasm about the project heightened her mood, which was a relief to Kavanagh. After having coffee, they walked the half mile to the Ocean House as the afternoon became cold and the sunlight slipped away.

At the hotel, Kavanagh suggested they stop in the Bistro Bar before going up to their suite. Lydia wanted to shower and change her clothes, so they went upstairs. As she prepared to clean up, Kavanagh, tired from their long walks, lay down and fell asleep. Upon waking hours later, Kavanagh was disoriented and surprised that the room was dark even though the drapes were open. He assumed Lydia was in the other room and stood up to find her. Instead he found a note that Lydia had left for him.

Dear Kavanagh,
I had a nice day with you and I did enjoy last night. When I asked you to come here to meet me I had left my friend in Providence who had become engaged and will marry soon. I was lonely and felt that I needed to be with you as you are a wonderful supportive friend. However after trying to be more than friends, lovers really, I found that it just does not work for me as I had thought it should. Once again, and

I'm so sorry, I will disappear from your life because I never should have contacted you with what has resulted in a false promise. You must forget about me as I cannot fulfill your expectations or your dreams. I wish I could. Goodbye dear Kavanagh my sweet friend.
Lydia

As he had done with Lydia's email message, three days ago, inviting him to meet her at the Ocean House as lovers, he read and re-read her note. While he was sleeping, Lydia had packed up her clothing and left the hotel. Kavanagh was terribly disappointed, but not completely surprised by Lydia's disappearance. The circumstances caused him to remember Florentino Ariza the patient soul in the classic novel, *Love in the Time of Cholera.* Ariza waited fifty-one years to claim the love of his life the beautiful and "naturally haughty" Fermina Daza. Author Gabriel Garcia Marquez characterized Ariza as having "the soul of a poet and the patience of a saint." Was Kavanagh doomed to a life without passion because he too had chosen to wait for the impossible, love and life with Lydia Merriman?

CHAPTER 15

Rayburn Office Building, Washington, DC

Since it was Wednesday, the Speaker's press conference was scheduled for 11 o'clock. Lydia was answering email messages as quickly as she could in order to be available when the Speaker had finished her remarks. The House Democrats were developing a bill that required members of congress to limit again all gifts and contributions from corporations, unions and associations in opposition to the Supreme Court's Citizen's United decision. Lydia was going to be interviewed as a sponsor of the bill by Joy Reid of NBC News at 11:30 in the rotunda.

Last night, unable to sleep, Lydia had been going over in her mind the list of targets from the recent meeting of the Knox group. It was a wide ranging list that included a former Secretary of State with far-right convictions, white evangelical racist beliefs, and presidential aspirations who was rallying support of the insurance industry to stop the Democrats' march toward Medicare for all. He was actually colluding with Trump in the development of a new cable network that was about to be funded by wealthy fascist-leaning Republicans. Trump, however was not ready for prime time as he had grown even larger, his hair white and a tic kept his facial features moving.

A Satmar Hasidic rabbi, who exercised almost life and death control over a thousand people and was immune from law enforcement due to the fear of politicians to become involved with a religious community that voted as a single block, was also targeted. He was gathering sympathetic politicians through extortion and bribery to support his desire to be granted a large section of federal land for his religious state. He argued that the Native Americans and the Mormons had been granted similar tracts that they governed without any local control, which was fiction. The idea of a place that was separate, but within the United States, was aberrant and had to be checked, and his followers had to be relieved of their near slave status by relieving them of the Rabbi's presence. And the warden of a Louisiana prison whose brutal methods were ignored by the governor and state legislature was added to the Knox group's list.

A former California congressman who without any shame had consistently lied and cheated on Trump's behalf had been unanimously selected for the group's attention. He had regularly attacked fellow members of congress who were conducting investigations into Trump's numerous and brazen crimes. And now the congressman had inherited the western share of right-wing wealthy and other dangerous people who no longer looked to Trump to install their agenda. His ability to appeal to those people with his nonsense had become a threat to democracy in California's delicate political climate.

Now the former congressman had mysteriously disappeared on his way to Santa Catalina Island to speak at the annual secret conference of the American Legislative Exchange Council held in the Catalina Casino, a distinguished art-deco auditorium opened in Avalon in 1929. The Council produced hundreds of model laws for Republican state legislators to enact in their states. The newly enacted state laws would devastate labor unions, rewrite tax codes, undo environmental protections and take action toward undocumented immigrants. The former congressman had sailed on a private yacht from Los Angeles to Catalina, a journey of twenty nine nautical miles, however, when the craft docked in Avalon's harbor, he was not aboard.

The event was reported on the evening news with great fanfare providing unwanted public exposure to the Council that had worked in anonymity for decades. Lydia, always startled when learning that the Knox group's work was carried out, hoped it would end soon. How many can we kill, she asked herself?

As she was about to leave for the rotunda, Lydia's desk phone rang and Connie the receptionist who screened in-person visitors said, "A Dr. Ruiz is here and insists that he must see you."

"Connie, I'm on my way to a TV interview. I don't know Dr. Ruiz." Lydia was annoyed until Connie told her that the doctor said they had met during a conference at Knox College. Lydia was stunned. She felt as if the temperature in the room had suddenly fallen. Moments later Connie ushered the Knox group member Lydia had dubbed "the Scientist" into the congresswoman's office. Attempting to get over her shock, Lydia asked Connie to call Betty Morris, Joy Ann Reid's producer and apologize for her not showing up for the scheduled interview. "Someone out there," pointing to the general office, "has Betty's number."

"Congresswoman, I'm Carlton Ruiz," He handed her a business card that showed he was professor of applied physics at the Massachusetts Institute of Technology. Also handed over was an MIT faculty photo identification, and a federal Security Clearance card indicating that his status was Top Secret.

Lydia was astounded. "What are you doing here?" she said while standing behind her desk? "You know we're not ever to contact each other. This is very dangerous. You must leave right now." She had become angry and wasn't at all sure what she should do about her visitor.

"Congresswoman, please be calm. I had to see you today. I'm not here to see the Capital. Can we please sit down? I have to tell you something that's important. I would never violate the rules." Lydia, disoriented by the presence of her surprise visitor, nodded and sat down. Ruiz took the chair on the desk's side close to Lydia. He spoke quietly. "I'm leading a team of scientists for the National Science Foundation. We're spending the next year at the North

Pole measuring, evaluating and experimenting in order to actually determine the damage to the polar cap, and to find the path to save the ice and the earth." He hesitated, and said, "I don't mean to sound dramatic, but it's true, we will be searching to find the solution in order to try to undo decades of climate change."

"Dr. Ruiz, I respect what you're trying to do. Of course I do, but why are you here?"

Ruiz looked directly into Lydia's eyes, and quietly he informed her that the reason he broke protocol today and was seeing her directly was that he had been the Zodiac the secret interface between the Knox group and the gang of the deadly skilled people that carried out the designated murders. He hesitated allowing Lydia to absorb the information. "And, because of the artic project I'm no longer available for the Knox group's work." He stopped speaking and took a deep breath before continuing. He was obviously distressed. "Therefore, Congresswoman Merriman, I have the duty to inform you that you have been designated the Zodiac."

Lydia's initial reaction was, "Who sent you here today?" Then she angrily said, "I will not be the Zodiac, I don't know anything about the Zodiac, and I'm finished with this discussion. Leave me now or I'll call the Capital Police and have you escorted out of the building." She thought if he left at once the Zodiac situation would leave as well. However, realizing that it really wasn't possible to avoid hearing what Dr. Ruiz had to say to her, Lydia reluctantly relented, calmed herself and said, "Okay, I'm not happy, but I'll listen. Tell me what this is all about."

Ruiz sighed, his shoulders dropped. "Congresswoman, this isn't easy for me. I'm a scientist. I'm devoted to preserving the environment in order to improve life everywhere. Now I'm involved with taking the lives of people who are threatening to destroy progress. Not only social progress, but the condition of this planet. I know we had to make the decisions we made, but it wasn't something I was prepared to do. None of us were, I'm sure. And my role became more complicated because I was the connection to the people carrying out the decisions made by the Knox group."

Lydia looking a little bit sympathetic said, "Dr. Ruiz I didn't know, actually didn't want to know, how the missions were accomplished. Whenever I heard that someone we had targeted was killed I tried to forget that I was a part of the decision that took a life. I've been able to do that up until a few minutes ago when you walked into my office." With her head back she looked to the ceiling not knowing what to do about being drawn even deeper into the scheme to take lives of people threatening democracy. "All right, say what you came here to tell me. I don't have much time, but I'll listen."

Ruiz looked around. Clearly he was uncomfortable. "Congresswoman Merriman, I don't think we should begin that conversation unless you have more time and we won't be interrupted. Perhaps I should come back here later today when your meetings are over and the office is quiet."

Lydia after taking a deep breath said, "Dr. Ruiz, come by my place tonight about eight. I live in Columbia Heights. We won't be disturbed. And considering the situation, you can call me Lydia."

After writing down the address, Ruiz said, "Please call me Carl. Only my parents ever called me Carlton. I will be at your door at eight." He stood, and for the first time in Lydia's memory of Ruiz he actually smiled.

True to his word, Carlton Ruiz pressed the door chime at Lydia's townhouse that evening exactly at 8 pm. To Lydia's surprise, Ruiz handed her a small bouquet of flowers when she opened the front door. He wanted to explain. "The flowers were sold to raise money for something in front of the pharmacy a block down. I think they were scouts or something like scouts selling the flowers. I hope you don't have hay fever and like flowers."

"I love flowers. Especially when someone gives them to me." Lydia stopped abruptly. They were meeting to discuss a deadly serious topic. It was not a date. However Carlton Ruiz was more sensitive than she had thought. Based on his limited interactions at the Knox meetings, she had believed he was a cold scientist, but right now he appeared to be nervous around her. "Well let's get to work." She led the way to the living area asking Ruiz if he wanted anything to drink. He didn't.

Ruiz was impressed with Lydia's home, and told her that he liked the art on her walls and the Nakashima table. "I haven't gathered fine objects. I enjoy them, but haven't had the time or really the inclination to acquire much of anything. Ten years after completing my doctorate I was still at Cal Tech, a faculty member, living like a grad student. I have a real apartment in Cambridge, but after almost twelve years there it doesn't look like much."

They sat on the new oatmeal color sofa. Ruiz opened the briefcase he carried and took out a cell phone. "This is a throwaway phone," he explained. "Here are five more. I bought them at Walmart for cash. Use them only once to make a single text, then dispose of them carefully. This is the number you use. You have to enter a code which changes every time you text." He explained the process that brings up the proper code each time, and how the phone card is removed before getting rid of the phone. Lydia made careful notes while thinking about where to hide them.

"OK, I get it. What else do I have to do?" She seemed to have resigned herself to the new role she was to play.

"You simply enter the subject's name on the text and some specific data that definitely identifies him or her. Such as date of birth, position or address. We don't want a mistake." Lydia nodded. She kept reassuring herself that the Knox group couldn't go on much longer.

"Now, this is the serious part." Ruiz looked at Lydia with pain showing in his eyes. She wondered what could be more serious than marking people for death. "Have you asked yourself about the manner that the sentences were carried out," he asked. Lydia nodded slightly almost afraid to hear any more. "Well," Ruiz continued, "Some people died quietly in a hospital for instance or by drowning in their pool. But, others, the really evil ones died violently by being dropped from a helicopter to the pavement or impaled on an iron church fence."

Lydia was afraid she was about to pass out. If she had been standing, she would have dropped to the floor. "Look Doctor, I mean Carl, I'm going to get a drink of water. I need it. Actually wine will be better. Will you join me?"

Ruiz agreed and Lydia left the room heading for her kitchen. She grabbed the first bottle out of the wine rack without looking at the label. A corkscrew and two glasses for red wine were gathered and she headed back to the living area. Lydia handed the wine bottle and opener to Ruiz who accepted the objects as if they were part of his usual activity with Lydia. The wine, a good Italian red was opened and poured. They didn't touch glasses. The occasion was too solemn for toasting.

"This is where the asterisks come in." Ruiz hesitated, he didn't want to shock Lydia, but she had to know this part. "Once a name is entered on the text message, one or more asterisks are added right after the name and before the background material." She took a big gulp of the wine knowing that what she was to hear was something she never had thought she would have to deal with.

Ruiz went to touch his wine glass, but something made him stop. "Lydia, I'm really sorry about all of this. Believe me please. I didn't pick you." He went on to explain the significance of the asterisks. The asterisks are the code that determines the severity of the action taken. For instance, one asterisk signifies a fast quiet death, two asterisks call for a more public demonstration such as falling from a window in a tall building." He hesitated. Lydia's eyes were focused on him. "Three asterisks calls for extreme measures because the evil that was done was so great. For instance being thrown from a helicopter or as the Fox News people found out, being beaten to death while hanging upside down in one's own office."

Lydia interrupted saying, "I thought he died of asphyxiation."

"The coroner's report says the deceased died of trauma from blunt force. What that actually means is he was beaten to death using the team signed baseball bat kept in his office." Now Ruiz needed the wine. "All right, last one. Four asterisks were used only one time.

That was Alex Jones impaled alive face down on the church fence." Ruiz was emotionally exhausted, and he fell back against the couch cushions as if seeking a place to hide out for a while.

Lydia didn't say anything. How could she do this, she asked herself? Finally she said, "I have a question. Who decides the number of asterisks used each time?" She thought, there must be a process. But who in the Knox group was the diabolical planner of death by degrees?

Ruiz remained quiet. He was carefully admiring Lydia's grace and elegance. She projected power and was obviously beautiful. He was falling under her spell as had so many men before him. However, he worried that what he was about to say would cause her to throw him out of her home before they had a chance to talk about anything not related to the Knox group. Would they ever get to know each other? Jesus, what was he thinking? He gathered courage and locked eyes with Lydia. He simply said, "You will."

Lydia's response was involuntary. She abruptly had stood up, and was almost yelling, "God no, I can't. I won't do any more of this." She turned on Ruiz loudly accusing him of selecting her for the deadly role she was expected to play. He begged her to believe that he had nothing to do with that. Instead of her anger growing and coming between them, after a moment, they hugged and comforted each other.

As they broke apart and sat again on the sofa, Ruiz was the first to speak. "Lydia, I'm not going to try to comfort you. There's nothing comfortable about the work we do. My only hope is that it'll be over soon and what we had to do has benefited the nation." They were sitting close together. Ruiz put his hand lightly on Lydia's shoulder. "I would like to stay in touch with you while I'm away. I'll have email but not cell phone service. Perhaps when I return we can get to know each other better. The circumstances will be different by then." They moved closer and kissed passionately, broke apart and kissed again.

Lydia, smiled slightly when they separated. "Carl, that was nice. I like you." She sighed, "But we can't see each other again.

Considering what we have had to do, we can't stay in touch. We'll have to forget each other's names and faces." Ruiz was about to protest, but Lydia's manner made it obvious that she would not change her mind, and that the evening and their brief affection was over. He rose, knowing Lydia was right. He kissed her forehead, picked up his briefcase and left.

CHAPTER 16

Kavanagh's Dilemma, July 21, 2023

M illicent's text to Kavanagh three days after their lunch meeting read: "I had a new contract between us prepared, and
sent over to your attorney Ken Fern as instructed. Please note that
our agency's rate of commission was raised to 12.5%, and that you
have agreed to participate in the promotion of the property, *The
God Myth*. The contract spells out the extent of your participation.
If your attorney has any questions, he should contact me directly
rather than our legal department."

The raise in the commission rate surprised Kavanagh especially since in the past, during their marriage, Millicent's agency
didn't charge a fee to represent him to publishers. He realized, of
course, that Millicent could no longer justify to her partners working for Kavanagh gratis. He decided he would casually mention
his promoting the book to Lydia at one of their Saturday morning
meetings. Kavanagh wasn't concerned about Lydia's reaction to
the book's republication since upon reading *The God Myth* several
years ago, she was complementary. He put it out of his mind and
returned to working on some of the most pressing issues generated by constituents. Lydia didn't return to her district for another
two weeks. During that time, the gears of big publishing and giant
media began to mesh and the campaign to produce and promote
Kavanagh's book was underway.

Attached to Millicent's email message was Kavanagh's tentative schedule for promoting his book on television news and lifestyle programs.

Interviews

Tuesday 9/5 Los Angeles ABC7 Eyewittness News Interviewers: Ellen Leyva, Rachel Brown
Wednesday 9/6 Los Angeles NBC Today in LA Interviewer: Sasha Pershing
Friday 9/8 San Francisco CBS KPIX Interviewer: Elizabeth Cook

Monday 9/11 Seattle KINGS 5 TV Interviewer: Joyce Taylor
Tuesday 9/12 Seattle KIRO 7 TV Interviewers: Michelle Millman, Monique Ming Laven

Thursday 9/14 Denver KPTG7 TV Interviewer: Molly Hendrickson

Monday 9/18 New York MSNBC Interviewers: Nicole Wallace, Lawrence O'Donnell
Tuesday 9/19 New York CNN Interviewer: Anderson Cooper
Wednesday 9/20 New York ABC TV Interviewer: George Stephanopoulos

---

The new edition of Kavanagh's book *The God Myth* was released after only forty five days in production. Prior to the digital age, book publishing was a complicated process taking over one year to turn out a hard cover volume ready for marketing and distribution. The ease of publishing a new book became obvious during the time of the Trump White House. Staffers at all levels who left the daily chaos and criminality inspired by Trump and his family members immediately wrote tell all books about their experience.

The books, and there were dozens, were made available at Barnes & Noble and on Amazon almost as soon as the author's resignation or dismissal was announced. Page layout and editing software absorbed the "authors" stories as they were being written or spoken. The editing programs *Scrivener, After the Deadline* or *Ninja Essays* organized the material gathered from Trump's "Adult Daycare" as the White House was characterized by one of his early chiefs-of-staff. Graphic designers using *Adobe InDesign or QuarkXPress* then created the book's interior in a matter of a few hours. Cover's usually consisted of a photo of the author and the title.

Kavanagh's initial book tour as outlined in Millicent's memo was scheduled to start in two months. He hadn't said anything to Lydia Merriman regarding his temporary absence from her staff, but he was entitled to a vacation, and considering their past relationship, he didn't expect her to object since he was giving plenty of notice.

It was a Saturday morning that found Lydia home in Millbrook. Kavanagh dutifully arrived at her front door promptly at 10 am with bagels and vegetable cream cheese, his laptop and notebooks ready for a work session. Lydia had made a pot of Starbucks' French roast coffee, and they sat at the large round table in her kitchen. While Kavanagh was putting his poppy seed bagel and cream cheese spread together, he casually said, "Oh, Lydia I'm going to need some time away in September. Millicent has been negotiating in my behalf with the publisher of *The God Myth* and the book will be re-published with an added hundred page introduction that I wrote some time ago."

Lydia expressed surprise. "I didn't know you were still in touch with Millicent. Of course, why would I know that?"

"Yeh, I agreed to promote the new edition, and the publisher is paying me the back royalties that have been tied up for several years. I expect a big check, but after taxes and Millicent's agency's commission I don't know what will be left for me. That's what I want to talk with you about. In two weeks, I'm scheduled to appear on some TV news shows to promote the book. Interviews have been set up in California, Seattle, Denver, and of course New York." He handed a copy of the interview schedule to Lydia.

She read over the places and times of the appearances. Her face showed she was troubled. "Kavanagh, let me understand this completely. You're going on prime time television in some of the hottest markets in the country and promoting your book that claims to prove that God does not exist. And you will be doing that while being identified as my district director responsible for constituent relations and my link to all organizations, local governments, religious leaders and anyone who wants to bring an issue to the attention of Congress."

Yes, but—," Kavanagh began to say.

Lydia interrupted him. "I can't believe that you expect me to accept the fact you're travelling around the prime time TV world as my senior staffer promoting atheism. You know I don't care about your personal beliefs, but my constituents will care. Your book tour will be used against me by the Republicans from now until I'm defeated in the next election. It's a gift to them. All of that ugly mob will suddenly become ultra-religious and accept Christ in their lives while sinning and stealing at the same time. They're hypocrites, which seems to be acceptable in our politics, but you will be labeled a heretic, my heretic, which isn't acceptable."

"Lydia, it's not that bad. My book is a comment on Western thought and philosophy. It doesn't call for the tearing down of churches or for any action for that matter. You read it when it was first published. You know I didn't intend to radicalize anyone."

Lydia had opened her Mac and was looking for a file. "I saved the *Times* review of *The God Myth* from 2015. Read it again and then tell me that the people who vote for me will be happy to have this publicized and thrown in their faces by the right wing media nuts."

"I know what it says. I'm flattered you kept the file for so long, but I don't think it matters. Read the review. It's sort of middle of the road. Millicent at the time was hoping for a fiery condemnation of the book, but that didn't happen. Please read it." Lydia turned the laptop back to herself and began to read the book review.

The New York Times Book Review
September 20, 2015

God Has No Religion
By Peter Daniels

Is it necessary to question God's existence? Is it logical to accept as a fact that a supreme force created everything and directs our lives and thoughts and actions? Is there a God for Christians, another for Muslims, Jews, Hindus, Jainists or Buddhists? Perhaps God is "local" catering to the needs of separate groups of believers, which is an argument for why the many Gods of Mount Olympus were found in ancient Greek myths. But obviously, that's no longer the case.

The God Myth
By Dr. Kavanagh, Henry Holt & Co. *445 pages Cloth $24.95*

Of course, the existence of God can be debated. Everything that can't be proven is subject to questions. Belief, however, is not scientific. Accepting the Trinity of Christianity is an exercise of faith. Accepting the tenets of religions has to be done blindly, but with full intelligence and the ability to allow for questions that cannot be answered or provided with proof of factuality. In his seminal work, *The God Myth,* Dr. Kavanagh a professor of social work at the City University of New York postulates that man created God. He professes that extensive examination has proved an absence of evidence of worship of a God or God-like deity in the surviving structures of the Scottish village Skara Brae. The community had existed from 3180 to 2500 BCE and didn't embrace a deity-centered culture, which was different from all other ancient societies.

Skara Brae is located in the Orkney Islands of Northern Scotland. Known as the Scottish Pompeii, its houses and storage buildings are well preserved as well as the inhabitant's furniture and remarkably enough the indoor plumbing that led to a sewage system. Dr. Kavanagh, on leave from CUNY, is currently the Chester and Margarite Goldman visiting professor of social thought at Setoncliff University. He has conducted extensive research of the many ancient communities in which evidence of discrete versions of worship was uncovered. However, in Skara Brae, the Picts people were shown to be family-centered and not involved in any manner with ceremony, worship, veneration or reverence to a deity. Due to the isolation of Skara Brae, and its complex small society, Dr. Kavanagh has made a case for the denial of the existence of God. Is the evidence produced by one remote small culture enough to draw the conclusion that God was made up by early peoples? I don't know. Anthropologists have developed other theories with less evidence.

British author Christopher Hitchens in 2007 published *god is not Great* a literary sensation that angered all of the Abraham religious leaders, something that should be done occasionally in my opinion. Hitchens, rather than questioning the existence of God as has Kavanagh, based his volume on claims that the result of religion is racism, tribalism, bigotry, ignorance and that it is coercive toward children and contemptuous of women. This dovetails with Kavanagh's meticulously researched theory that states unequivocally that God was created by the ancients in order to control women in the primitive societies because males were required only for procreation. I don't agree or disagree with Kavanagh, but his theory is intriguing. His scholarship is evident, and perhaps it's time once more to examine what it is that can better help human beings live their lives based on a belief system that nurtures and protects all of us. God, if she exists, has no religion and neither do Hitchens and Kavanagh and perhaps they are correct.

Peter Daniels, SJ is professor of world religions at the Berkeley Jesuit School of Theology.

After reading the book review, Lydia addressed Kavanagh as if she was a prosecuter. "The review contains enough evidence to scare any of my God-fearing constituents away. It's clearly an indictment of religion, which will anger anyone especially those who feel guilty because they don't go to church. Religion has been mixed in with politics in this country since the white evangelicals seized control of governments in the southern states making religious observance a means test for holding public office."

She hesitated before saying what she didn't want to have to say to Kavanagh. "You have to understand. By promoting your book, it will spill over on me. I'm trying to do good in Congress for women, immigrants, poor people, the disabled. You know all of this better than anyone, and you also know that because of the subject of your book, and your being affiliated with me will possibly cause me to be defeated in the next election by a Republican who hates all of the people I'm trying to help. You can't really believe that your book won't be used against me. I'm really sorry Kavanagh, but I can't accept your plan. You may not promote your book while a member of my staff. You have to decide between the book and continuing to work with me."

Kavanagh was dumfounded. He wasn't prepared for Lydia's reaction. Once again he had underestamated her. She was willing to end their working relationship and their personal history together. Looking hurt and defeated he said, "All right Lydia. You don't have to fire me. I resign." He began to pack up his notebooks and lap top. "I'll leave the notes for my successor." He smiled slightly. "You would think that I would have learned something from your rejecting me twice before. But I've been in love with you for half my life, and always hoped you'll need me and want me to be with you. I finally get it. It's not happening, you and me, and now we can't even work together." Lydia didn't say anything. By resigning, Kavanagh had done what had to be done. For that she was grateful. She didn't want to hurt him. He always was a careing friend. Without looking at Lydia, Kavanagh turned away, and after picking up his coat, left feeling disappointed and broken hearted.

CHAPTER 17

Sussex County, New Jersey

Tommy Grimes or as he preferred, Pastor Tommy sat in the choir loft of the former Presbyterian church in Harley, New Jersey. Grimes was shirtless and drinking his second bottle of Bush beer at 9 am. The white clapboard church had been closed for over twenty years, not unusual for the once-popular Christian sect that if still operating was likely to be sharing its premises with a brand of Korean Christianity. Currently it was rented to the Aryan Nation Christian Alliance as proclaimed by the plywood mounted sign outside. Tommy Grimes was frantically texting and Tweeting putting out the word that the national leader of the Oath Keepers had accepted the invitation to speak at the church on Sunday.

Grimes was a self-appointed pastor. He hadn't attended a seminary, in fact, he barely graduated from high school, but he could sure talk. The older residents of New Jersey's most western county referred to him as a spellbinder. Some of the county's white evangelical Christians actually remembered the revival tent crusades that found their way to rural New Jersey in the 1960s, and Grimes was favorably compared to them.

The Oath Keepers were founded as an anti-government organization as a reaction to the election of Barack Obama, the nation's first black president. The organization's membership is secret, but it's estimated in the tens of the thousands. Members are former armed services veterans and retired and fired law enforcement officers who show up at public places heavily armed and pretending to act as back up to local police authorities. The founder, a graduate of Yale Law School, was delusional and paranoid believing that only by arming the citizenry would they be protected from black and brown people taking over the white Christian American society, after all hadn't there been a black president who was also without doubt a Muslim?

The federal government, he believed supported programs that disadvantaged the white population and resistance was in order. The current leader of the Oath Keepers was even crazier, and openly called for the establishment of a fascist, white citizens' state in place of the Constitution. Felix Dembow, the leader had grand pretensions regarding expanding the Oath Keepers to the northeast.

He believed that by establishing a foot hold in New Jersey, even in the poorest, least populated, and most western section of the state, New York was next. He was sure that New York was controlled by Jewish, homosexual, black loving Communists, and it was his mission to protect the rights of the good white Christian Americans in New York where they were outnumbered. Therefore he agreed to speak at Tommy Grimes' church in order to begin the Oath Keepers infiltration of New York City, and to pick up some promised contributions. Dembow was ignorant of the fact that Sussex County, New Jersey while only 63 miles from Manhattan might as well be a thousand miles from the city.

Dembow and his driver pulled into the old church's driveway at 1 pm arriving in a silver SUV with Colorado license plates. He figured they would get some lunch and some bourbon and relax before the 2 pm talk to the already packed house. Tommy Grimes was warming up the church members with a script provided by the Oath Keepers that would rile up an audience of white supremacist sympathizers.

A parishioner stationed at the front door waved to Dembow and then went inside the church to tell Tommy Grimes that the speaker had arrived. Grimes rushed to the front door to welcome his honored guest. As Dembow stepped from the silver SUV, shots rang out from three places, and he, fatally wounded, fell to the ground. His driver, afraid to move, slid below the seat hiding as best as he could. Grimes ran back into the building screaming that Dembow was shot.

In only a few moments, parishioners armed with assault weapons stormed from the church. With Grimes' encouragement, they had showed up at the Aryan Nation Christian Alliance armed with military grade weapons, illegal to own in New Jersey, but readily available for sale just ten miles away over the Delaware River in Pike County Pennsylvania. The good God-fearing folks, armed with semi-automatic AR-15 rifles and Mac 10 assault pistols, sprayed the woods across the street from the church with high capacity ammunition.

As the group moved toward the trees while continuing to shoot blindly, precise gun-fire was returned and the church members began to fall hit by skilled snipers. The silver SUV provided some cover and parked as it was in front of the building's entrance allowed the survivors to retreat into the church. When the shooting stopped, the SUV's driver slipped out of the vehicle and ran down the road that led to town. He was not seen again.

People who had remained in the church while the shooting was underway had called the nearest New Jersey State Police barracks in Frankfort Township. Calls then went out from the barracks to nearby hospitals in Pennsylvania, New York and local communities. In about twenty minutes, medical personnel began to arrive and tend to the wounded and state police officers covered the dead after collecting their identifying information.

New York State troopers from a nearby barracks were summoned by New Jersey officials. They arrived on the scene cordoning off the area, and began a search of the woods from where the shots originated. Once the area was secured, the damage was evident. The result of the fire-fight was seventeen dead, including Felix Dembow, and eleven severely wounded. At one point, FBI

Special Agents arrived at the scene from Newark by helicopters to access the situation and evaluate if the attack was in fact terrorist inspired.

A search of the woods and surrounding areas revealed two elevated places where shooters had stood and had a clear view of the church entrance, and one spot on the same level as the church that was splattered with blood. A trail of blood ran from that spot between two oak trees to a narrow road about a hundred and fifty feet behind the woods. Police theorized that a vehicle had been parked on the black top surface and a wounded sniper had struggled to get to it. It was likely that the barrage of bullets from the church members' guns had hit one of the assassins. Nothing else was found at the three kill sites. No bullet shells, cigarette butts, footprints. Nothing except broken twigs and blood.

While police were trying to make sense of the horrific event that took place in rural New Jersey, a black Ford Explorer was being driven just slightly over the speed limit on Route 84 to Scranton, Pennsylvania and then south on Route 81 to Memphis, Tennessee. The Ford's driver would stop only for refueling on the sixteen-hour drive. A passenger slept on the rear seat and in the far back, the team's third member lay dead from gunshot wounds.

News of the shooting traveled quickly. By nightfall all of the news programs carried reports on what was called, "The Massacre in New Jersey." Clearly it was unintended. The assassins' mission was to kill Felix Dembow putting a stop to the national aspirations of the Oath Keepers. They had been sent to Sussex County, New Jersey by the Knox group's directive to eliminate one dangerous individual not to kill sixteen others.

The FBI, news media people, politicians, and federal terrorism analysists were baffled by the killings because Dembow wasn't on their radar, and theories were put out, rejected, and new ones appeared. On an NBC news report a spokesperson for the ATF informed the public that most of the weapons used by the church goers were AK-15s, and because the Colt Arms Company in 2018 suspended the production of that model for "personal use" it had become the most desired weapon for ownership by the gun nuts. However, Lydia Merriman knew the reason for Dembow's assassination. She had ordered it with one asterisk.

CHAPTER 18

Peekskill, New York

The following morning, while the metropolitan area was still reeling from the shooting at the former Presbyterian Church in New Jersey, Kavanagh after reading a complete review of the deadly event in the *Times* brought out a spiral notebook. He listed from memory the unsolved murders of notable and notorious people.

From the *Times* article that day, Kavanagh learned that the previously unknown Felix Dembow was a disbarred lawyer from Nevada. He was affiliated with radical white supremacists calling themselves the Oath Keepers. It wasn't clear from the newspaper's account why Dembow had driven to western New Jersey the day before, but as the article's author pointed out, he was killed in an obviously planned ambush, which had turned into a mass shooting.

Reporters had found Dembow's place of residence in Nevada. They interviewed Dembow's odd-appearing fiancé, a retired social science professor from New Jersey. In a strange irritating voice she said that if she had known Dembow was going to her former home state, she would have gone along. Kavanagh took out his laptop and brought up news articles about the other killings that have remained mysteries. After reading a dozen news items, he

107

discovered a thread among the murders on the list that appeared to be so obvious it made him wonder why reporters hadn't picked it up.

He turned off the computer since the morning was rapidly coming to a close and Millicent was due to arrive there around noon. They were discussing Kavanagh's recent TV appearances to promote the new edition of *The God Myth,* and development of a series of programs set in the still available places of the ancient world. As was usual for him, Kavanagh's refrigerator was empty of anything except condiments. He had promised to provide lunch for Millicent who was on her way to Peekskill in an Uber.

Kavanagh picked up his iPhone and called Nonna's Restaurant in Peekskill. He liked the traditional Italian menu offered by the eatery located in a small strip mall. He ordered a green salad accompanied by grilled salmon, flat pasta with pesto and chicken, a portion of sautéed broccoli rabe and for desert cherry cheese cake. The restaurant promised to deliver the hot lunch in thirty minutes.

At 12:15, Kavanagh's phone rang. It was Millicent who had arrived at the condo complex and found it confusing. She was actually in front of Kavanagh's unit and he walked outside to greet her. "Kavanagh, every place looks alike here. I feel like I'm in a new version of Levittown. How do you find your way home?"

"Welcome Millicent, nice to see you again." They went inside and Kavanagh opened a cold bottle of Left Coast Cellars Pinot Grigio. "Our lunch will be delivered soon. I wanted to wait until you were here so it will be hot." Ten minutes later the doorbell rang and their lunch arrived. They talked business while eating the restaurant's food. Millicent was impressed with the selection of dishes that had been prepared by a restaurant so far from Manhattan.

She had brought a check for the royalties owed to Kavanagh by the publisher that had been tied up in a dispute for five years. He had expected the payment to be about $170,000, but the check from Magna Carta Literary Agency, Millicent's company was in the amount of $86,260. When Kavanagh complained about the amount, Millicent handed him a statement showing the expenses that had been deducted from the original amount Kavanagh's book had earned.

MAGNA CARTA LITERARY AGENCY, LLC

Statement

The God Myth (Kavanagh)

Royalties $172,000

Commission @12.5% $21,500
Federal Tax @20% $34,400
NYS Tax @10% $17,200
NYC Tax @2% $ 3,440
Legal Expenses $ 9,300
Total $85,840

Net Amount $86,160

Kavanagh was surprised, not in a good way. "Really Millicent, this is all I'm being paid for my research, my writing and doing that damn series of TV interviews that cost me my job with Lydia Merriman."

"Kavanagh, I don't understand. Does that mean you're not on the congresswoman's staff?

"That's exactly what it means. Lydia couldn't take the chance of being associated with someone trying to prove that God doesn't exist except in the minds of people controlling other people."

"I'm really sorry. I know how much working with Lydia meant to you, but, the TV interviews were the only way to free up the money owed to you and get the new edition published."

"I understand that, but I owe almost half of the check for back alimony to the first Mrs. Kavanagh, and my legal fees amount to over $10,000. I'll pay off the car I just bought, and there will be just enough left for dinner at Gramercy Tavern."

"Oh, poor Kavanagh, everyone's against you. You'll be paid royalties for the new edition and I've worked out a deal for you with an educational TV channel to host a series on ancient civilizations and their worship customs. Now tell me about the interviews."

"All right." He opened a second bottle of the Pinot. "The interviews in California and Seattle went as well as expected. All of the interviewers were women and we got on well. They like anything out there that goes against the established norms. In Denver, I felt like a novelty. Are you really an atheist, they asked? Back in New York, I felt challenged. Now that they don't have Trump to report on hour by hour the networks have returned to in-depth news analysis. Nichole Wallace was great. Smart, sexy with a big sense of humor."

Millicent commented, "Of course you liked the women."

"I also liked Lawrence O'Donnell at MSNBC. I've long been a fan of his 10 o'clock news show at night. Do you know that when Mitt Romney was running for president, O'Donnell said that Romney came from a religion founded by a criminal who was anti-American, pro-slavery, and a rapist? He also said that the Latter Day Saints was a made up religion quickly put together by Joseph Smith in order to distract his wife after he was found having sex with their house maid. The Mormons were not amused, even though it's probably true, and O'Donnell to his credit apologized."

"Millicent smiled, "You Irishmen stick together."

"Millicent," Kavanagh retorted, "Your English roots are showing. The British government tried to starve the Irish for two centuries. They almost succeeded. That's why there are so many Irish in America. We had to leave to survive. It's the same story as every other immigrant group that came here without anything, and against the odds built good lives for their families."

"All right, no more lectures. Let's talk about the offer from the Discovery Channel."

"Yeah. What is that again?"

"It's the Discovery Channel. They......discover things. You know that. Its science and other stuff. It'll be all right. Look, they have a sponsor for a ten-part series. And you don't have to go anywhere. They'll shoot the footage and you'll provide a commentary in front of the scenes as if you were actually there. It will work, and you'll be paid well, as will I."

"Okay," he conceded. "Set it up. I need something to do, something to look forward to now that I'm unemployed. By the way, I'm doing it only if Discovery is different from the History Channel. Have you seen those morons on that *Forged in Fire* mess where they make bigger and sharper knives and hack up sides of beef? It's really disgusting. How the hell do they justify that crap?"

I don't know, so don't worry, no knives. I'll send the Discovery contract to you, or should it go to your lawyer?"

"No, send it to me. I can't afford more legal bills." They had finished their business and Millicent had begun packing up her papers. He asked, "How will you go back to the city. I can drive you to the train."

"Thanks, but I have an Uber coming here in fifteen minutes. By the way, what about that shoot out in New Jersey yesterday? You know, I think there's some sort of plot going on. Lots of fascist types are getting killed. What about that?"

CHAPTER 19

Knox College, Galesburg, Illinois

It was December, and Lydia was unhappily on her way from Chicago to Galesburg for a meeting of the Knox group. It had snowed recently, but the roads were clear, sanded and salted. She thought of the assembly of her fellow patriots, meeting to mark undesirable people for extinction as the murder bureau. She had been depressed since receiving the latest summons to Galesburg, which was slipped into in a Hallmark Christmas card and was mailed to her. Lydia needed to pick up a cup of coffee before she reached the college's campus. The group's standing instructions forbade entering the college's cafeteria or any other place except Old Main the historic building where all of the group's meetings took place.

Leaving the highway, Lydia had a choice of fast food establishments and unaccountably she chose a Popeye's' chicken restaurant. The famous chicken sandwich on a brioche bun was now regularly available for purchase after two years of being sold out immediately all over the country as soon as it was offered. Lydia ordered the fried chicken without mayonnaise or pickles and a cup of coffee with half and half. After two bites of the sandwich it landed in the trash bin, but the coffee was soothing and Lydia finished it before driving to the campus.

The notice of the group's meeting included the usual instructions. It had been three months since they had been summoned to Galesburg and Lydia wondered nervously whose names will be presented today. She always rationalized that the group's mission was necessary, actually vital to maintain the nation's core values, but she also wondered how the Framers of the Constitution would have reacted and would have any of them approved.

She parked the Hertz rental, a Ford Fusion, which drove smoother than her Jeep Cherokee. After leaving everything she was carrying except the car's entry key, Lydia walked up the steps of Old Main. Lincoln had debated here and eventually took the nation to a war against itself. Even his critics agreed he saved the Union, but at a terrible cost that to this day wasn't forgotten or forgiven by people living in the states that had comprised the old Confederacy. Would Lincoln have approved of the Knox group's mission and its decisions? She suspected he might have approved since he arrested dissenters against his war, and chased an anti-war congressman to Canada. He had unfriendly journalists held in a jail on an island in New York City's East River.

The meeting room was quiet. Four other members were there and Lydia was almost expecting Carlton Ruiz to attend and explain his leaving the group. That would have been the normal behavior of a member of an organization who was leaving, but there weren't any other organizations similar to the Knox group. The member Lydia thought of as the Professor had the electronic detection device on the table in front of him. The other woman in the group, the Advocate, gave Lydia a quiet, tired smile. The Philanthropist nodded and the Hippie ignored her. The Advocate said, "Let's get started. We're five now. I propose that we retain the two vote veto of proposed actions against selected subjects." Lydia wondered how she knew Ruiz had left the group, and did the Advocate know Lydia was now the Zodiac? The other members quietly agreed with the proposal, which meant that four votes instead of five were required for the taking of a life.

The Hippie was the first to speak. "I have inside relationships with the intelligence units of the Southern Poverty Law Center and the Anti-Defamation League. They're the best monitors of the white supremacist movement, the individual groups within that sick world, and the people who are emerging as leaders and the danger they offer for all of us." He stopped speaking as if waiting for the group's reaction, but no one commented.

"All right. Here's the deal," he went on. In about four months, next April 30 to be exact, American neo-Nazis, and their friends will celebrate the one hundred and thirty fifth birthday of their deranged hero, Adolf Hitler. Yet, it's hard to believe, but the tattooed freaks who make up the base of the far-right extremist world are over whelming the great grandchildren of World War two veterans who fought the Germans."

The Advocate, looking skeptical said, "So what. They have a drunken party for a day and then they go back to the rat holes they came from. Why should we care?"

"Because, the SPLC people discovered that a twenty acre plot of land was purchased in Yanceyville, North Carolina as the place where the neo Nazis will hold the Hitler party in April. They expect two thousand to attend. Actually Yanceyville's population is only about twenty-three hundred with over twenty registered sex offenders, which is about ten times the national average."

The Philanthropist broke in. "Well they have to be known for something."

The Hippie continued. "The land was bought for less than $3000 an acre by a company set up in Malta for the land purchase. It's impossible to uncover who actually owns the property. Yanceyville is in the state's center. It's the county seat with a median income under $16,000. The Daughters of the Confederacy erected a monument there to the South's soldiers in 1921. They still don't know they lost the war." Lydia thought about what the President had said, the South had actually won the Civil War. Now she understood what he meant that day in the Oval Office.

The Hippie ignited with passion, continued his appeal to the Knox group. "The promoters of Hitler Day are lining up shit kicker bands, acts like Ted Nugent, purveyors of Nazi memorabilia, and sellers of anti-Semite and anti-Catholic literature along with hate-filled books and magazines that feature villains who are black people or immigrants. Of course, the day will also feature self-appointed white evangelical preachers to stir up the crowd. And they will be stirred up. Moonshine, meth and opioids will be the cuisine of the day."

The Advocate asked. "Won't law enforcement intervene since, the refreshment are all illegal?"

The Hippie shook his head and smiled tolerantly. "Do you really believe that the Yanceyville police force of six officers will actually confront a crowd of maybe two thousand drunk, high, heavily armed and full of hate degenerates? Besides the locals will no doubt welcome the Hitler lovers, it will be their fucking Woodstock." He stopped speaking and looked at the others around the table. Seeing no reaction he continued. "If this is permitted to happen, it will energize white supremacists everywhere. The movement will come out from under rocks and everyone who doesn't fit the lily-white image will be in danger. Hate crime will be ordinary. The nation will become a battle ground. It's the Trump legacy."

"So do you have a proposal," the Professor asked?

"Yes, yes I do. I propose that the entire collection of Hitler lovers be wiped out. Machine guns, rockets, grenade launchers whatever it takes to be rid of all of them. They'll be fenced in and unable to escape and they'll be even more brain damaged from the meth and pills. It's an opportunity that won't happen again. If we don't act, the next time they all meet up to celebrate another attack on morality and decency they'll have loads of security. Probably the North Carolina state police will protect them or the United Daughters of the Confederacy will patrol the perimeter."

Lydia was shaken. "Are you serious?" She asked with distain. "You want everyone killed who shows up at Hitler day? What if there are families there? Children, wives who are victims because they have to live in that sick culture. Do you want to kill all of them?"

"You haven't seen the opportunity here. Some of the worst of the white supremacy hate crews have already signed up to attend the populist gang bang. It's going to be tremendous. Because we're prohibited from having any paper with us, I'll attempt to tell you the names of the vermin that so far are expected in Yanceyville, but I may forget and leave some out." He took a deep breath, looked up at the ceiling and began to list the assemblies of sociopathic failures who inhabit more places in the United States than one would suspect. "Fourteen of the twenty six Ku Klux Klan's still operating in our fair nation will be represented, perhaps with their entire membership. The Aryan Guard, the Proud Boys, Redneck Shop, Christian Identity, the Aryan Brotherhood, the Red Shirts and not to be forgotten the hosts and organizers the American Nazi Party." He stopped speaking and looked at his four colleagues, then asked, "Well are you impressed? And there will more, lots more when the word gets out and they find gas money to get there." He was emotional now. "They must be stopped. Yanceyville, if we intervene will be their Waterloo."

The room was quiet. No one made eye contact, and no one spoke. Finally, the Philanthropist broke the silence. "Look I appreciate your intentions. Yes, the people you talk about are despicable and I can't understand how they think especially since their relatives three generations ago fought and died to defeat Hitler. It's sickening to see their web sites showing Nazi arm bands, German SS gear and signs that say Six Million More. How do you think I feel as a black man when post-cards celebrating lynching from the 1930s are sold on- line by these deranged white supremacists? I'm sure they'll also be for sale at Yanceyville."

The Hippie spoke up. "That's why we have to act and order an attack on that obscene event. Using drones, gas the entire place. No one will even know what happened. It's far enough out of town so the residents won't be harmed." He stopped speaking to gather his thoughts. "It's beginning to appear on their god-dam website *Stormfront.org.* Tune in and you'll see it growing."

Shaking his head, the Professor said, "Enough, we are not killing acres of people. I can't believe you even brought it up. A recent assignment from this group caused the death of sixteen other people. Yes, they all were armed with military grade weapons, and yes they opened fire on the men carrying out our mission, but only a single individual was the target. If this collection of Nazi's actually happens in Yanceyville there will be so much media coverage that anyone attempting to stop the hate carnival with force will not be able to come near it. Every house near there with indoor plumbing will become an Airbnb for TV crews." He stopped speaking, looked around and said, "I vote no, anyone else?"

Panic was developing in Lydia's mind. I will not order an attack on in Yanceyville. I won't do it. She actually knew that practically everyone who will show up there on April 30 hated her and everyone she represented simply because she was different from them in appearance. Lydia was highly successful in the television industry, a member of Congress, educated and from a stable family. She was everything they were not, but in the eyes of the neo Nazis, she was just a black woman, and she had no place in their world. But, who would want to live in their world of poverty, ignorance, addiction and life spans that ended early by death or imprisonment?

Lydia certainly hadn't any desire to get to know the people who were judging her. She didn't care about their living conditions, the lack of education or having no chance for satisfying careers. Lydia believed that the strange underclass dedicated to hating the people they don't know or understand had willingly made the choice to ignore the opportunities of the greater society.

While the Hippie spoke, Lydia was silently obsessing about her role in the process of carrying out the group's decisions. After the Professor made his opposition to an attack on April 30 known, she realized that by adding her no vote the Yanceyville massacre would be avoided. She was relieved, if only for the moment, but still she felt some comfort. Lydia was constantly reviewing the debacle in Sussex County, New Jersey that took sixteen lives and severely wounded many more. Her angst had prevented her from functioning in her usual efficient manner and was disrupting every night's sleep.

The fact that all of the causalities were firing illegally owned military grade weapons blindly into woods not knowing if uninvolved people were nearby and in danger, hadn't soothed her guilty feelings. Lydia had retreated into her thoughts forgetting, for a moment, where she was and what was transpiring around her. She suddenly realized that the group was waiting for her vote, and quickly she said no making four votes against the proposal to decimate with deadly force the future gathering in Yanceyville, North Carolina organized to celebrate the most monstrous individual of the 20th Century.

Some other names were carefully brought up, and discussions ensued. They were people whose actions were regularly causing disruption of the democratic process, and somehow were immune to legal process or social pressure. The individuals put up for discussion by members of the Knox group that day included a daughter-in-law of Donald Trump, a former United States attorney general, a shirt sleeved congressman who remained unindicted for his part in a sex scandal at a major public university, and a senator whose father may have been a collaborator in the assassination of John F. Kennedy along with others less well known. Some of the names received unanimous votes to be acted on others were passed over.

CHAPTER 20

It was Saturday morning and Kavanagh allowed himself a single well done poppy seed bagel schmeared with vegetable cream cheese that he picked up at Kurzhals Coffee, located in an old repurposed industrial building in the center of Peekskill. He no longer felt inhibited by ordering only a single bagel. He was becoming tougher. Perhaps being sacked by Lydia Merriman four months ago, and travelling around the country hawking his book at Barnes and Nobles, university book signings, and Ethical Culture Society author nights were reasons for the new persona. Or was he just tired of being taken for granted especially by the women who had wound their way through his life?

Actually Kavanagh was bored. He had retired from college teaching. About that he was happy because grading papers and exams no longer interested him. Even advising students regarding their education and careers was something Kavanagh didn't want to do anymore. He didn't understand the change in his focus since moving from Manhattan to a place in the Hudson Valley, but it was a fact: He was standing still for the only time in his adult life. Millicent had promised a project for Kavanagh on the Discovery Channel, but that was bogged down. No one had called him for consultation on the ancient history series. Millicent when he asked her said that the funding was held up. Had it been a ploy to get Kavanagh on the road to promote his book? Yes, he had collected the royalties that had been held up by litigation, and Millicent's agency had also been paid.

As he gazed out over the bay that connected to the river, Kavanagh enjoyed the fresh bagel and two cups of black French roast coffee. He couldn't help comparing the morning to all of the Saturdays he shared bagels and coffee with Lydia at her home. Just being in her presence was pleasurable. He adored watching while listening to Lydia explain her position on an issue. Of course she had changed from the young competent gorgeous woman she had been when they had first met to a mature competent gorgeous women who was in charge of everything around her. And, yes, she rejected Kavanagh's desire to become close to her, in fact several times, but in some remote part of his mind, he believed Lydia would reach out to him again and he would happily shed his pride and eagerly embrace her.

Since returning from what Kavanagh described to his two adult children over dinner one evening as his "road trip," he almost constantly thought about what the future might hold for him. After all, he was only in his mid-sixties, in good health and living comfortably in a pleasant place with great water views. He had privacy since he didn't know any of his neighbors, and most important New York City was accessible by a good rail line. Whatever friends he had lived in the city either in rent controlled West Side apartments or in condos they had bought long before the New York real estate boom made ownership of Manhattan properties impossible for members of the middle class.

One night while on the road trip Kavanagh was at dinner in Los Angeles with Sasha Pershing, who had interviewed him for the NBC News program. He rolled out his feelings of frustrations since retiring, and what he should do with his life. They had finished taping the interview around 6 pm at NBC, and Pershing suggested they have dinner together. She was the television station's religion editor and conducted the rare interviews that touched on religious issues. She was an ordained Episcopalian priest. "Sasha," Kavanagh asked, "What do you call a women who's an Episcopal priest? I can't call you father."

"That's a small problem we have. Actually we don't have a term for us. I respond to Deacon or Sasha, just don't call me mother." For their dinner she had suggested the California style Italian restaurant, in West Hollywood, Olivetta, which offered a lush setting and modest noise level so they could talk easily and stay as long as they liked. Most of the city's newer places for dining were minimalist in décor. Glass and stone combined with stainless steel allowed sound to bounce off every surface. The noise levels were high and constantly on going no matter how populated. Conversation was impossible, but that didn't seem to matter since everyone was using cell phones.

"Have you always been an Anglican, or are you a fallen away Catholic tired of the sins of the hierarchy and the church's scandals?" Kavanagh asked?

"Yes, I'm a cradle Episcopalian, and studied to become a priest after my husband died eight years ago. I had some small parts in films a long time ago, but wasn't noticed." Sasha had the presence of a dancer. She moved about with elegance, back straight and head up, and was about the same age as Lydia Merriman. She was attractive with gray hair worn in a feathered pixie cut. Sasha had conducted a competent taped interview of Kavanagh for NBC, which would be on the air the following day at 8 am and 6 pm, the station's primary news hours. After listening to Kavanagh's case against religion and the very existence of God, Sasha defended the desire and need of most people to follow something that provided comfort and solace specifically during the troubling times of their lives. Her justification of the spiritual mystery especially of Christianity was passionate, but not argumentative.

Kavanagh was not as polite. He pointedly asked, "Why does Christianity lend itself to so many phony false profits that promise healing, wealth and salvation?" He continued before Sasha could answer. "That's been going on here for a century. Billy Sunday, Aimee Semple McPherson, Mordecai Ham all claimed they had the key to the Promised Land. The evangelicals and their circus tents moved around the Mid-west selling cures to disease, sight to the blind, and any other miracles the suckers were willing to accept. They had people howling like wolves, spouting nonsense which they called speaking in tongues and throwing away their crutches as they fell down."

Sasha was able to interrupt Kavanagh's chronical of revivalism in early 20th Century America. "I agree that some of the practices of the revivalists were questionable, but they did bring the message of the Good News to the prairie states and who knows how many continued to live Christian lives after being converted? In fact Billy Sunday is credited with a million and a half conversions to Christ."

Kavanagh couldn't resist adding, "And what about the new crop of TV evangelical preachers spawned by decades of the success of the 700 Club's artfully prying money out of little old ladies? They can't afford their medications, but regularly send checks to Pat Robinson to pay for his family's expensive life style and to provide employment for his son so that he never will actually have to go to work."

"Look," Sasha began, "I minister at the LA jail two days a week with people waiting for trials and I actually see some of them repent and promise to change after they accept Jesus, and we can believe them. I give out bibles which for many is the only book they will ever read, and they're grateful. I know it makes a difference or I wouldn't be doing it."

Kavanagh's response was unyielding. "You have no proof that any of it has done any good. You're a pretty woman. Is there a man in jail who would not love your company? I believe it's immoral to spread religion among vulnerable people. They need solid assistance, help with solving their basic problems, not some pie in the sky."

Sasha didn't respond so Kavanagh continued with his opinion of the evangelicals. "Of course the greatest huckster of all was Billy Graham who became rich and politically influential from his crusades. In the 1950s he spent twelve weeks in England attracting the lower classes to his performances much to the chagrin of the Archbishop of Canterbury who spoke of 'the menace of fundamentalism.' And presently son Franklin Graham is trying to duplicate dad's accomplishments. However, Franklin is anti-gay and anti-Muslim and who knows what else Franklin is against. Didn't Jesus say, 'Love your enemy,' I think he did?"

In spite of their differences, they were enjoying Olivetti's baked Branzino and Bucatini pasta with cashew pesto. Sasha asked Kavanagh, "What are you, a recovering Catholic? You seem so angry about religion, I assume you were a mistreated altar boy."

"No, that's not me. I'm an Irish Jew." When Sasha's expression showed surprise, Kavanagh continued. "My mother's family immigrated to Ireland in the late 1800s, and my dad's just after 1900. They were part of a migration from Latvia in Eastern Europe, a place called Lita in Yiddish and were Litvaks. Those Jews followed others who had migrated to Ireland for decades, about five thousand in total. No one knows why they came to Ireland originally, but they were welcome there, the most Catholic nation.

Most of the Jewish population that didn't leave that region in Europe was decimated by the Germans by 1940. Don't think life was easy for Jews before the war. They were identified and singled out for abuse by almost everyone in Poland, Ukraine, and Russia and throughout the Empire of Austria-Hungry." Emotion showed on Kavanagh's face. He knew that if his grandparents hadn't left Lita, they probably would not have survived. "Our name was originally Khadorkov. My mother's father was Robert Briscoe the famous Jewish Lord Mayor of Dublin and a member of the Irish legislature for almost forty years. My parents moved from Dublin to New York in the 1940s, after the war. I was born there. In fact until recently I've not lived anywhere else."

"So you gave up Judaism," Sasha asked.

"Oh, no. You can't give it up. It would be like saying, I'm no longer Chinese or French. You can move somewhere else, and even become a citizen of a new place, but you can't give up ethnicity. Because Jews weren't citizens of the places where they lived in Eastern Europe their ethnicity was their Jewishness. That has changed somewhat with most of the world's Jews living in America and Israel. I feel comfortable describing myself when I need to do that as a Jewish atheist."

"I see. At least I think I see. Kavanagh are you married, divorced, living with someone, gay, bi?"

"I've been married and divorced twice," he answered. "I have two grown children whom I see regularly and so far two wonderful grandsons." He hesitated before going on. "I'm hopelessly in love with a woman with whom I've slept with twice in thirty years. I know that it sounds crazy, but that's the effect she has on me. We didn't see each other for twenty-five years in between. And to make it even worse, until recently, I was a member of her staff.

She's a congresswoman and she fired me because of this book tour I'm on right now." When Sasha looked confused, Kavanagh explained. "I was her district director. I set up her local appointments, saw constituents and supervised the two district offices. But a member of a congressional staff giving TV interviews promoting his book that denies the existence of God was too much to accept for any politician. I had to go. We haven't spoken since."

Sasha's reaction was, "I need another drink." She signaled the waiter and ordered two Beiraos on ice. "It's a Portuguese liquor with a slightly mint taste. You'll like it." She covered Kavanagh's hand with hers. "Does this all mean that you don't see other women, even women who live far away and aren't seeking a relationship, just some affection some night?" She looked at Kavanagh directly as if to challenge him to reject her now or agree to spend the night together.

Kavanagh trying to keep Lydia from his mind said, "The night is young. Let's see how it goes."

CHAPTER 21

St. Louis, MO

The headline of the story below the fold of Sunday's *St. Louis Post-Dispatch* read, "**Is the Deep State Confronting the Rightists?**" An article written by two long time journalists for the distinguished mid-west daily newspaper claimed that an organized conspiracy exists, which has eliminated scores of individuals affiliated with extremist right-wing causes.

John Younger and Victoria Hope Pulitzer Prize nominated writers found a path of evidence providing speculation that a silent movement is underway that uses murder to silence "enemies of the state beyond the reach of the legal system." While the article didn't identify anyone who may be involved in the conspiracy, the writers had interviewed people who had offered information and some proof of collusion.

Victoria Hope had been approached by a resident of the St. Louis suburb of Ballwin, Ava McGill, a young widow who sometime soon after her husband's funeral became suspicious and wanted to know more about the cause of his death. She had believed that her husband, Ray McGill, was a highly paid structural steel worker due his Mohawk heritage, and lack of fear of heights. Ray traveled around the country installing, he claimed, the beams that topped out skyscrapers. A call from a company in Memphis, Tennessee informed Ava of Ray's death from an accident on the construction project where he had been working on the open steel. The caller, a woman, expressed her condolences admitting that she hadn't known Ray. And she asked that Ava, when able to do so, call back with the name of the funeral home to which, Ray's body would be sent. The cost of the funeral would be borne by the construction company, and the company's employee life insurance plan would pay a benefit to Ava. Nothing else had to be done since the death certificate was issued in Memphis and had already been submitted to the insurance company. The call ended leaving Ava afraid, depressed and without her husband.

Ray McGill had served in the U.S. Army in Iraq, but not as a Ranger or a member of the Special Forces. McGill had applied to the elite units after basic training, but was rejected after failing the test for physical stamina. Instead he became a truck mechanic, which was a valuable service for the Army battalions stationed at Camp Victory in Bagdad. McGill served two tours in Iraq without becoming involved in actual warfare, but earned a sharpshooter badge for accuracy, and was mustered out of the Army 1n 2015. He maintained his interest in weapons and spent every Saturday, back in St. Louis at a gun range perfecting his shooting accuracy.

At home Ray worked as a mechanic for a Caterpillar tractor dealer. He was cooperative and worked without complaining, and was considered a competent employee. He led a quiet life, between his work and the gun range until his cousin's wife introduced him to her best friend Ava Korsco. They immediately enjoyed each other's company and fell in love. Ava and Ray married a year later, purchased a small home in Ballwin, a suburb of St. Louis, and in 2018 Ava gave birth to twin boys.

The director of the Ortman-Stipanovich funeral home called Ava and informed her that Ray's remains had been brought to the facility from Tennessee, and would she or her representative please come in for positive identification and make the final arrangements. Ava was still in shock since being informed of Ray's death just three days before. Her parents moved into Ava's home to take care of the boys and Ava alternated between sobbing and sleeping. Her brother Don was dispatched to the funeral home to make the positive identification of Ray's body and arrange for the wake and burial. Next, Don met with their family priest Father Jerome Cassidy, pastor of Holy Infant RC Church in their parish to schedule the funeral mass three days hence. They selected music for the choir and readings to be offered by Ray's sister, cousin, and Ava's dad Antoni. Don and his wife Alice would participate in the funeral mass by bringing up the offertory gifts.

A week after Ray's funeral, Ava was home and the twins back in kindergarten with the teacher and school nurse carefully observing them. In mid-morning, the doorbell rang. It was the postman with a certified letter that Ava had to sign for. Distracted by thinking about Ray, and that she knew nothing about the circumstances of his death, Ava put the envelope on the dining table along with the stack of other unopened mail. Later that day, Ava's mother, Greta, tidying up the living room and dining room asked, "Shouldn't you open some of this mail?" Ava just nodded. Greta sorted the stack into three piles, junk mail, sympathy cards, and bills. The certified letter went into the bills pile. "Ava, do you want me to open the bills and some official looking stuff?"

Her daughter agreed, and Greta using a letter opener began to open the statements and bills until she came to the certified mail envelope. The return address was *Pacific National Life, La Jolla, CA.* After slitting open the envelope, Greta pulled out the single small insert. One look at the contents of the envelope made her sit down abruptly. Unable to speak, Greta handed the single piece of paper to Ava who stared at it and then said, "I forgot about this." Ava examined the printed document which turned out to be a check for $500,000 made out to her. "I think I remember the woman who called to tell me about Ray said something about life insurance, but I couldn't think about it. I still can't. What should I do with it?"

The check from Pacific National Life was deposited in a branch of Citizens National Bank, and was cleared three days later. Ava, who had never been financially independent before didn't question the source of the insurance payout. If she had wanted to locate the company that sent her the half million dollars she wouldn't have found them in La Jolla, California since the temporary post office box there had been closed. In reality Pacific National Life was only a checkbook kept by an attorney in an office over Sharkey's Bar on Grand Cayman Island in the Caribbean.

Greta convinced her daughter to inquire about other insurance that might be paid out from Ray's union the International Association of Bridge, Structural, Ornamental, and Reinforcing Iron Workers. Ava couldn't deal with talking to the union about her husband's death so Greta from her home one morning called the union's main office in Washington, DC. What she learned from the pension and benefits department of the giant international union was something she couldn't share with Ava, at least not yet.

Two months passed by and Ava was adjusting to widowhood. She hugged her sons more, and thought wistfully about the happy times with Ray. Everything he had owned or used was left where he had them. She couldn't stand thinking about cleaning out Ray's closet or moving the tools that were all over the garage. Ava had decided to return to St. Louis Community College where she had studied graphic arts for two semesters. She dropped out when the twins were born, but now had the means to return to college. Ray's cousin's wife Janet who had introduced Ray to Ava was an assistant registrar at the college, and was elated when she found out that Ava wanted to continue her education. She urged Ava to attend a talk by a reporter for the *Post-Dispatch* on women returning to college in order to enhance their lives. The reporter, Victoria Hope was scheduled to speak one week after the beginning of the new term. However, Ava was confronted with two issues related to Ray's death prior to her registering again as a full-time student.

On a Wednesday morning, Ava received a call from Farther Cassidy, pastor of Holy Infant RC Church, the celebrant of Ray's funeral mass. The priest asked if he might stop over for a short visit one day soon. When Ava asked what this was about, the priest answered that it had to do with Ray, and perhaps Greta could be there as well. The priest came to see Ava with Greta in attendance on Friday morning. Ava brewed a pot of coffee and served a walnut coffee cake ring from Bello's Bakery. Father Cassidy appreciated the cake and coffee, but was clearly unhappy about being there.

"What I'm about to say has troubled me since Ray's funeral. I discussed the issue with the Bishop and he was adamant that I had to tell you." Ava and her mother became even more puzzled. Cassidy continued, "When Ray's mass was over, I rode to the cemetery with Tom Pierce, the funeral director. During our time together, Tom, who I have known for about twenty years, and consider an ethical and honest man, told me the following." The priest hesitated knowing that what he was about to say to Ava would have a life-changing effect. "Tom said Ray's remains arrived at Ortman-Stipanovich at night. The driver was alone and helped remove the heavy casket from his vehicle. It turned out that Ray was incased in an expensive metal casket. Tom offered to give the casket back, but the driver refused and left immediately. Ray had been embalmed. Your brother brought clothing for Ray when he arranged for the wake and burial. When Tom's staff dressed Ray it became obvious that he didn't die from a construction accident. He died from two gunshot wounds in his chest."

At first Ava was dumfounded, questioning, then she fell apart crying loudly and moaning. Greta embraced her daughter not knowing what to do to comfort her. Father Cassidy stood up and said, "Ava, Greta, I'm sorry to have brought this news to you, but you had to know the truth. I wish I had an answer for you, but only God has the reason. Please believe that your faith will help you through this tragic time." He put his coat on and assured the two women that he was immediately available if they needed him.

Greta waited two days for Ava to recover from the news brought by Father Cassidy. She worried that what she was going to say would also have a disastrous effect on her daughter. What she had to tell her was that her call to the structural steel workers' union revealed that Ray was not a union member and never had been one. Also it was not possible for him to have worked on major construction projects in the nation's cities without union membership.

CHAPTER 22

Kavanagh was back in New York. He had reluctantly left Los Angeles and Sasha Pershing, but he had interviews scheduled on CBS, MSNBC, and CNN, all located in Manhattan television studios. He didn't love California, but he really liked Sasha Pershing. He wondered about families that lived in different parts of the country or even other parts of the world. His children and grandchildren lived less than twenty miles from him, and he saw them regularly. Could he, should he, break away from the east coast and perhaps find a happier life somewhere else? It wasn't a question he wanted to answer right now.

He had plenty to read, back copies of the *Times* delivered upon his return home, and some books ordered from Amazon. However, he decided to do some research on events that had been troubling him for a while, actually from before his book tour. Also, he had recently heard a short TV news report that quoted a *Post-Dispatch* article about a suspected plot to deal harshly with left-over Trump democracy deniers. Digging around online, he found the story from the St. Louis paper, which was speculative and didn't mention names, but hinted about a left-wing conspiracy, but without proof or validation.

Kavanagh opened his laptop and sorted through a year and a half of *New York Times* reports on the series of homicides of people known to be far right on the political spectrum. He found the half year old story on the Senate leader's death, the massacre of ten

ARA people, Steve Mellor's drop from a helicopter two hundred feet over Manhattan, a personal favorite, and about two dozen other unsolved cases. The deaths of these dangerous individuals didn't really disturb Kavanagh, but he found a pattern among the timing of the murders in clusters about three months apart that disturbed him greatly. He decided to go to St. Louis and talk with the reporters who wrote the article.

Victoria Hope and John Younger were elated by finding what they believed was a thread that fit into Ava's story. Younger, a former Marine, had purposely spent some time at the shooting range where Ray McGill had practiced. He had struck up conversations with the range's owner also a former Marine. After the Semper Fi exchange they spoke freely one day when Younger finished his drills with a licensed pistol. At one point, Younger asked the range owner if he remembered Ray McGill. "Yes, of course I do," exclaimed Kevin Richards. "Ray came in here all the time for a couple of years. In fact, he met the guy here who recruited him for the high steel jobs that eventually killed him." When Younger showed surprise, Richards said, "Yeah, I know the guy was ex-CIA or something like that. I wondered why he was looking for steel workers. It didn't fit, but Ray told me he had signed up to do some work that the guy offered him, for serious pay."

Ava McGill had met Victoria Hope after her presentation at the community college women's event. They agreed to meet at a downtown Starbucks the next morning. Ava related Ray's story as she knew it: the insurance payment, Father Cassidy's revelation concerning Ray's death and what the structural steel workers union representative told Greta. Ava also admitted that Ray had earned a great deal of money over the last eighteen months, more than she had realized. Did structural steel work pay that well, she wondered? Victoria pressed Ava to recall when Ray had been away from home during the last year and a half. Ava had entered Ray's travel dates in her calendar book in which she also kept doctor's appointments and play dates for the twins so she knew the exact times when Ray said he was traveling to a construction job.

Victoria went on the hunt for more facts. Her associate John Younger had been reassigned to another breaking story so she was on her own as far as the Ray McGill story was concerned. First Victoria contacted the Memphis health department asking for a copy of Ray's death certificate, a public record. She was informed that no proof of death for a Ray McGill had been issued by the department since his death had not been reported to them. Victoria then contacted every health department in the counties that surround Memphis, with the same result. She called the funeral director who had received Ray's remains. No paper-work accompanied the body, he said, as permits were not required to transport a corpse from state to state. The funeral director would not speak about Ray's wounds, and referred Victoria to Farther Cassidy. The priest assured the reporter that everything he knew about Ray's death had been relayed to Ava and her mother.

Kavanagh decided to contact Victoria Hope. She agreed to meet with him when he told her of his interest in her theory regarding the systematic elimination of far right people who threatened the democratic process. Kavanagh explained his research, and Victoria was impressed with his tracking of the murders. He felt he had to go to St. Louis to talk in person with the reporter to try to find out why the string of killings was happening. He packed for a short trip, flew to St. Louis and the next day they met in her cubicle of an office at the newspaper. The *Post-Dispatch* was founded by Joseph Pulitzer in 1876 when he merged two St. Louis daily newspapers. It had one of the last classic newsrooms, and the paper had been headed by a member of the Pulitzer family until 1995.

Victoria moved a pile of papers from a chair, and Kavanagh sat down. "So," Victoria began, "You're the famous Dr. Kavanagh. I read your book when it first came out." Kavanagh waited for her negative criticism. "I loved it," Victoria continued. "I believe religion and politics are the same. Both dirty businesses, and your theory that the concept of God was invented by the ancients in order to control women is brilliant and right on the money." Victoria Hope had covered St. Louis for a long time. She had been a Miss

Missouri right after college three decades ago, and had competed in Atlantic City for the Miss America title, which led her to a career as a journalist.

They exchanged the information each had collected. Kavanagh had created a detailed spread sheet with all of the murders, the places, and the dates that he believed were planned and carried out by a group of conspirators who were heavily financed and had some sort of official sanction. Victoria shared everything she knew about Ray McGill's death and why she thought Ray was somehow connected to the string of deaths on Kavanagh's spread sheet. "I have his travel dates, and, praise Jesus, they align with the events on your spread sheet. Not all of them, but enough to draw the conclusion that Ray was involved in some serious shit."

CHAPTER 23

St. Louis, MO

B ack at his hotel, Kavanagh thought about the day and was
pleased with the time he spent with Victoria Hope at the newspaper. They shared information, theories, and speculations, and
they planned to meet with Ava the next day if she was available.
As it turned out, she was free mid-day so a lunch meeting at the
Hilton Hotel by the Arch where Kavanagh was staying was set up.
The historic hotel building had been a nineteenth century monu-
mental bank building that had been artfully turned into spacious
comfortable hotel rooms. Even the bank's massive steel and brass
walk in safe had been incorporated into the hotel's barroom.

They met in the hotel's lobby restaurant. Victoria made the
introductions. "Ava this is Dr. Kavanagh. He's a social psychologist
who's working with me as a researcher on our project." Ava smiled
and nodded. She was a slender woman who obviously was unhappy
and seemed unsure as to what she was doing in a restaurant with
two people she hardly knew.

During the night prior to seeing Victoria Hope, feeling alone
and not really sure what he was doing in St. Louis, Kavanagh called
Sasha Pershing in Los Angeles. He was surprised when she said, "I
almost gave up. Why did you take a week to call?" He explained
that he had been thinking about her, a lot, but became involved in
a project that required his immediate attention and had to travel.

"Okay, Kavanagh, I'll forgive you. Where are you?" When he said he was in St. Louis, she asked, "What's going on there?"

"I can't explain right now, but I think it's important that I'm here." He thought for a moment before going on. "Have you been to St. Louis? It's my first time here. It's actually a pleasant city." Sasha admitted that she hadn't spent any time in the Midwest except for two visits to Chicago. "Well how about flying here for the weekend?" He was elated when she immediately agreed to meet him, and promised to call back with the time her flight was scheduled to arrive Friday afternoon.

Sasha's Southwest Airlines flight to St. Louis took about three hours and twenty minutes and arrived at 4:10 pm. Earlier in the day, Kavanagh and Victoria Hope had met again with Ava this time at her home in suburban Ballwin. Victoria had asked Ava to call her bank and ask for copies of the deposits made to hers and Ray's joint checking account. In fact, Ave went in person to the nearby bank branch. A bank officer explained that because the deposits in Ray's name were made by wire transfer, traditional deposit slips didn't exist and the amounts shown in the monthly bank statement were the only records available. Kavanagh had said, "I'm not a lawyer, but I believe you can sue the bank, and quite possibly you'll be able to have the court issue a subpoena for the information you're seeking." When Ava indicated her reluctance to become engaged in a law suit, Victoria assured her that the lawyers for the *Post-Dispatch* would handle everything, and all Ave had to do was to sign some papers. The meeting ended without a plan. Victoria agreed to stay in touch with Ava and share any new facts surrounding Ray's death that may be uncovered.

Kavanagh was early. Sasha's flight was shown online to be on time, but he was feeling anxious, so he took the hotel's shuttle to Lambert International Airport arriving almost an hour before her flight was due to land. Sasha was among the first passengers to enter the terminal from the Southwest plane. She pulled a small Hartman hard-side suitcase along until she spotted Kavanagh. They hugged and kissed with a passion that belied the fact that they had seen each other for the first time only a week ago. They Ubered back to St. Louis. Sasha was hungry so they stopped at the Mud Café for coffee and some appetizers consisting of hummus and goat cheese on thin toast points to hold them over until dinner. Kavanagh had made an 8:30 pm reservation, the only time available, at Café Natasha's, a fine Persian restaurant in the Central West End with an enviable reputation for unusual cooking. Because of good reviews in newspapers and online restaurant sites, it was an achievement to score a dinner reservation on a weekend.

The next morning, in bed together, Kavanagh was happy, actually delighted, and told Sasha that he hadn't felt so good for a long time. "She smiled and said, "We aim to please. By the way, I Googled your congresswoman. She's impressive and very good looking." Kavanagh was surprised, and asked why she bothered to do that? "Because before travelling two thousand miles and spending a weekend with you, mostly in bed I suspect, it made sense to find out as much as I can about you. I Googled you before our interview on NBC.

I'm impressed, no make that thrilled that you, a member of the Anglican clergy, is willing to spend her quality time with an anti-religion atheist. And I have no secrets. You know about my marriages, and my children and grandchildren. I also have a sister two years younger who lives in Venice, Italy. Her husband is an international art dealer. That's about it. Now what about you? I haven't Googled you. I just forgot to do that. But should I?"

They were snuggling now feeling so good to be close together. Sasha began, "As you know, I have a daughter who is a speech pathologist at a hospital in San Jose. She lives with a Silicon Valley hotshot. Of course, I can't ever bring up marriage to her. Besides my two days ministering at the jail, I work the rest of the week in the development department of the Bishop's office. Basically I'm a fund raiser, which isn't easy as there are fewer and fewer members of our congregation. And on some Sundays I fill in for other priests who are ill or away. Prior to the seminary and ordination I hadn't worked at anything important since my short-lived film career. I was in some beach bikini movies and some other flics where I was always in my underwear," she smiled playfully. "There, you know everything there is to know about me. I hope you're not bored."

"On the contrary," Kavanagh couldn't resist saying as he pulled the sheet away from Sasha showing her nakedness, "I think the directors knew what they were doing."

"Very funny. All right, what else should I know about you? Two ex-wives and a congresswomen can't be the whole story."

Kavanagh thought for a moment before answering. "I like the company of women. I'd rather be with women than men. I don't fish, golf, bowl or hang out watching football and empting beer bottles. There were two other woman I had loved, but their circumstances made it impossible for us to be together for very long." He stopped, wondering if he should reveal more of his secrets to Sasha, but he never held back when it came to a women who intrigued him, and she was waiting for more details. "Oh, what the hell. I had a friendly relationship with a Catholic nun, a lovely woman, who was president of a university where I was a visiting professor. The relationship progressed to a single night's intimate experience, which was delightful until she left in the morning assuring me that she would soon forget what we had done."

"Oh, Kavanagh, that's a sad story for both of you. I've wondered about women and men committed to celibacy. Obviously there are exceptions, but it seems like a terrible idea. Now what about the other woman you loved and lost?"

"Yes there's one more, and I think you're enjoying this." He continued. "I visited Ireland several years ago. I told you my family is Irish. While I was staying in Dublin for a few days I met a friendly passionate woman who was a physician, a radiologist in a university hospital in Dublin. We connected emotionally right away. During our first dinner together prior to going to a concert, we discovered that we were first cousins and our mothers had been sisters. That was embarrassing. She was so upset she almost left the restaurant. We spent the next day together touring family sites. We had a nice time together, but when I called the next morning she said she didn't want to see me again. I was hurt and returned to New York earlier than I had planned assuming I wouldn't hear from her.

Six months later she came to New York for a medical conference, and called me. We met at her hotel and after a while, at her urging we went to bed. I was elated, but when I asked where we were as far as our being together, - - - I was ready to commute to Ireland, I was told she was returning to Dublin and I shouldn't contact her because her daughters didn't approve. I remember thinking that after having sex with a nun and with my cousin, I was definitely going to hell." He pulled a pillow over his head.

"Well it could be worse," was Sasha's reaction. "However, I'm pretty sure that after this weekend together I'm going to want to see you again, and you better want to see me." They got dressed, had breakfast, and the rest of their day was taken up with a visit to the top of the St. Louis Arch, six hundred and thirty feet in the air. Then a paddlewheel boat ride on the Mississippi made for a pleasant afternoon because it was an unusually warm early spring day.

As the paddleboat moved along the river known as The Big Muddy for obvious reasons, Kavanagh watched Sasha admiring her and wondering if she would become weary or disenchanted with him at some point. That was his history with the women he fell for, and he hoped that a relationship would develop. Would Sasha be different? He wasn't going to bring up anything about their future together if in fact they had a future together. Instead he asked Sasha about her life since becoming a widow. "Sasha, I'm wondering why you a smart and beautiful woman hasn't had a line of suitors begging for attention, or have you?"

"Kavanagh, that's a sweet way to ask why I'm haven't become attached to a man over the last eight years. You were in LA recently, right?" Kavanagh agreed. "Well,' Sasha continued, "There are more beautiful women per square block in Los Angeles than anywhere else in the world. And, they're all a third of my age. Does that answer your question?"

Later, in the evening, they found the one place in St. Louis where jazz was still played as it had been a century ago when it came to the city from New Orleans. They enjoyed being together dining on shrimp po'boys, red beans and rice and drafts of Red Stripe beer, all the while listening to the hot and cool music at BB's Jazz, Blues and Soups where they arrived late and stayed until closing.

Sasha's plane departed Lambert Airport for Los Angeles at 3 pm Sunday. Before she left him, Kavanagh had decided to come clean and tell her what his mission in St. Louis was all about. After explaining everything he knew and suspected, Sasha was concerned about Kavanagh's safety and realized the gravity of what he confided. Of course, she swore to keep it secret, but wondered why, Kavanagh, had become interested in what was a dangerous situation.

However, the reason he became involved in the first place was omitted in the explanation he had given Sasha. He would not admit it to anyone, but he suspected that in some manner Lydia Merriman was involved with the series of targeted killings of individuals, people whose actions were so harmful to the very establishment of democracy. Kavanagh came to this disturbing conclusion because he knew Lydia's schedule. When he worked for her it was part of his job as her district staff director to know where she was, and what she was doing at all times.

After checking on Lydia's calendar for the last eighteen months that was still posted on his laptop, Kavanagh discovered a pattern about three months apart when Lydia would disappear for two days. After each of those occurrences there were reports of deaths of dangerous people who freely operated beyond the law. Of course, it was gross speculation on his part, but there was a thread connecting the murders, not obvious, but one that bespoke of some sort of official sanction to rid America of the people who were leading the charge to destroy the Founders great experiment in freedom.

CHAPTER 24

Rayburn Office Building, Washington, DC

The appointments assistant in Lydia Merriman's Washington office was attempting to answer the congresswoman's question of why she was scheduled to meet for an entire hour with someone she didn't know or knew anything about. Connie, the assistant, a recent graduate of George Washington University nervously explained that the chief of staff of New York's governor had personally called to request the time with Lydia for Benni Zaiter from her district who was due to show up at the Rayburn Building office in about thirty minutes.

At the appointed time, Benni Zaiter strode into Lydia's private office, bowing slightly as they shook hands. His manner was continental rather than American. He was well attired in a dark suit possibly an Armani, and he radiated self-assurance. "Thank you for seeing me. I'm sure you have very full days, but what I have to say is important to your district. Up to now, the governor and his senior staff are the only ones outside of my company who know about our project, which will be important and significant not only to New York, but to the entire country." Lydia was obviously interested and a little anxious since she wasn't included in the discussions regarding a new major development in her congressional district. She couldn't help thinking that if Kavanagh were still her district director she would have known about Benni Zaiter.

"Congresswoman Lydia, please do not be insulted that you are hearing about us today for the first time. My company is Amerind Botanical. We are a solidly financed organization backed by some of the most important people in finance, technology, product distribution, and health maintenance. Our basic premise is that we are bringing back to the United States the manufacture of pharmaceuticals, the medicine we all use in some manner."

Lydia was relieved that the project was a simple business deal so she asked, "Why the secrecy? This is wonderful news, and I'm hoping at least some of it will be happening in the 18th Congressional District."

"Well as a matter of fact, we have purchased two hundred acres of land just east of Poughkeepsie for our manufacturing facilities. Also, we are closing on a four-story building in Poughkeepsie's downtown which will serve as our operations center until the manufacturing and research campus is completed. We wanted to have our plan solidly in place before the public announcement."

"I see, Lydia replied, "This is wonderful news. The potential for employment is substantial. Also property values will be enhanced, and the halo effect on small businesses, restaurants, retail stores will be quite positive. Do you need my help?"

Zaiter was smiling when he said, "Your endorsement will allay the fears of the naysayers who are always with us. I have asked around and you are highly regarded by everyone I have met in your district. The property we have acquired crosses some state and county roads, which will mean some detours and road closings while the construction phase is ongoing. Also the amount of traffic generated by our project, especially truck traffic will be significantly greater that what is now normal. Our major concern, however, is that we expect some backlash here in Washington because we intend to end the manufacturing of American marketed pharmaceuticals in India."

Lydia was surprised, but now she understood the project's goal. "Pharmaceutical manufacturing leaving India is the best idea I've heard in a long time. The fact that our medicines are primarily made in that filthy country has always troubled me." Zaiter had inadvertently hit upon one of the issues that Lydia was most passionate about. "India," Lydia continued, "is dysfunctional and disorganized. Its president, Ram Nath Kovind, has scapegoated the Muslims and Christians in India so that Indians will focus on their prejudices rather than on their poverty, hunger, homelessness and lack of sanitation or a chance for a better life. They don't seem to care about any of that. A tiny minority lives in regal splendor in India while the vast majority haven't ever improved their lives." Lydia, while with Ted Turner's company had traveled to India for the production of a documentary film. She wasn't prepared for the multitudes of people living, eating and relieving themselves on the streets of India. That picture held in her mind made it impossible for her to accept the production of medicine in that dysfunctional country, especially where sexual assault of women was commonplace.

"Yes," Zaiter was quick to agree, "But the many educated Indians who have migrated to America and joined the large technology companies compose a powerful block in the Republican Party. They were staunch supporters of Donald Trump, and represent the highest casts and are used to getting their way. They don't want our project to even begin let alone succeed. They have vested financial interests in keeping the manufacturing where it is."

"What can they do about it," Lydia asked?

"The majority of pharmaceutical purchases in the United States are connected with Medicare and Medicaid. The Food and Drug Administration has great power over the compounding of medicines. Congress passes the laws that govern these procedures. What is needed are new laws preventing the manufacture of medicine in sub-standard countries that do not properly oversee the production of life supporting drugs. The lack of serious inspections or the casual quality of the oversight of India's pharmaceutical industry may eventually result in a crisis of major proportion when drugs become ineffective or even deadly. Even companies like Bayer manufacture pharmaceuticals in India and Pakistan in unsupervised facilities."

"I think I see. You want me to sponsor a bill that has a chance of passing both houses, and then signed into law by the president. I'm a second term member of congress. Certainly I will support legislation that that benefits your company because it's a good cause. But you will need members and senators with lots more seniority and influence than me."

"I know all of that," "but," Zaiter responded, "I have to have you as the member of Congress from our district behind us. We will do the work of contacting your colleagues through the experts at firms here in Washington who will provide information to the Congress that is obvious to you and me, but not to everyone."

Lydia asked, "Do you live in the district?" She was surprised when she found out Zaiter lived in Spackenkill, a small hamlet in Dutchess County.

"Yes, last year I bought a stunning glass walled home built about forty years ago by a brilliant architect for his own use. It's on a rise so the views are wonderful. In fact, in three weeks I'm hosting the announcement of our project at my home. I also came here today to personally invite you. The invitation may be in your mail pile by now. Also it's important at the event that you publicly and strongly support changes in the laws that govern pharmaceutical manufacturing abroad." When Lydia's face registered concern, Zaiter said, "Remember, its India we're talking about. Not Canada, Japan, or Denmark."

The hour flew by and Zaiter, sensing his appointment was finished, because Lydia's desk phone kept ringing stood and thanked Lydia for her time. She in turn assured him that the establishment of Amirind Botanical at home was the best news she had in a long time. He hesitated before turning away to leave. He asked, "I enjoyed our talk and would like to prolong it. Will you have dinner with me tonight?"

Surprising herself, Lydia suggested they meet at Bresca on 14th Street North West. "It's a beautiful place, and the dishes are French and small, which I like. Let's say 7:30. My office will wrangle a reservation." He happily agreed.

CHAPTER 25

St. Louis, MO

Kavanagh enjoyed the hotel's extra-large bath towels. They were towels to be lost in while drying off from the shower. He was thinking about ordering similar towels for his bathroom at home. The towels he used there were smaller and weren't soft enough. They were left over from his marriage to Millicent. She was English and he suspected that the average English person didn't care much about the fluffiness of bath towels. When their marriage ended, Millicent left everything that their apartment held except for the few pieces of art she had brought to their marriage. The towels reminded Kavanagh that all of the furnishing, linens and knick-knacks filling the condo unit in Peekskill were left over from his second failed marriage, and perhaps it was the time to find some possessions he enjoyed.

While he was dressing and trying to decide when was time to leave St. Louis, Kavanagh's cell phone rang. "Kavanagh, its Victoria. I'll pick you up in ten minutes in front of the hotel. Lots of stuff is happening."

"Victoria, I'm still getting dressed, make it twenty minutes." Her answer was fifteen.

She picked him up at the hotel and they drove to Ava McGill's home about a twenty-five minute trip. Victoria was excited. "Yesterday the paper's lawyer called the chief legal officer of the bank. They were in the same Wash U law school class. After a conversation, the bank's lawyer agreed that Ava had the right as the co-owner of the account to see the deposit details. This morning, at nine o'clock Ava received an email from the bank. She called me and I called you."

"What did it say?" Kavanagh was curious about the message that got Victoria Hope speeding out of the city.

"I don't know. I told Ava not to forward it to me or to anyone else. Who knows if she's being monitored?"

This morning, Ava was more welcoming to Victoria and Kavanagh. She had coffee and Danish pastry for them. Kavanagh was relieved since he hadn't had time for even one cup of coffee before meeting Victoria Hope. Ava had printed two copies of the bank's email to her, and gave them to Hope and Kavanagh. They were surprised by the amounts that had been deposited in Ray and Ava's bank account. "Did you know about the deposits?" Victoria asked? Ava just shook her head. The printout listed seven deposits over the last sixteen months. They amounted to four hundred and twenty five thousand dollars. The deposits had been wired to their bank branch by Deutsche Bank in New York, and each had three letters and some numbers listed as well.

Victoria took the printout into the next room and sat at the dining table, her phone and pen out. After pressing in a phone number, she asked for Jeff Cohen. Moments later they connected. "Jeff, its Victoria Hope. How are you? Yes, it's all good. Jeff, I have to find out something about wiring money internationally. No, I don't want to send money to anyone. Yes, it's a story about money laundering." She waited until Jeff asked some other questions. "Jeff, I have a list of deposits wired by Deutsche Bank to a local branch bank here in St. Louis. Yes, Trump's former enabler bank. Yes, I'm also surprised that Deutsche is still in business. Here's what I have." Victoria recited a list of letter and number combinations that no doubt Jeff was entering into a software application. After a few minutes, Victoria began making notes on the email printout. When she finished she said, "Jeff, thanks very much. I'll be in touch."

Both Ava and Kavanagh were anxious to know what Victoria had learned. "Okay. Here it is. All of the deposits originated in either Panama, St. Lucia or Grand Cayman. They were sent first to Deutsche Bank in New York to ally suspicion that would surround money transferred from foreign banks to a suburban branch bank. Deutsche is actually an American charted bank so transfers from one national bank to another wouldn't alert the bank regulators."

Ava, appearing pale got up and picked up an envelope from the kitchen counter. "This came in the mail just before you got here." She handed Victoria the envelope which had the famous Holiday Inn logo on the left top corner. It was a form letter from the Holiday Inn in Memphis, Tennessee. The letter informed Ray McGill that the hotel had packed up his possessions that had been left in the room he had used. The hotel room had been paid for, so the letter was not a request for money, however the suitcase with Ray's possession would be held for sixty days in conformance with Tennessee law and if not claimed would be disposed of immediately thereafter.

While they digested the hotel's message, Ava thought of something else that had been overlooked. "Ray's truck, a GMC less than a year old is missing. I had forgotten about it, but the hotel's letter reminded me again that the truck is missing. I don't really care, but Ray loved that truck. He paid fifty-eight thousand for it, cash, and bought me the Volvo in the driveway."

Kavanagh thought for a moment and said, "Ava, I'll go to Memphis, if that's all right with you. I'll pick up Ray's suitcase and look for his truck. Ava looked at Victoria who nodded her agreement with Kavanagh's offer. "I'll need the truck's license plate numbers and the keys." They left Ava and headed back to downtown St. Louis. "I'm going to try to get a flight tomorrow morning to Memphis. I'll get in touch with you when I get there."

"I wonder why," Victoria asked, "Deutsche Bank threw in with Trump? He's caused them a lot of trouble."

"Well, it's like this. Deutsche was trying to gain a foothold in the New York real estate development market when they first opened up there. The bank's directors, all Europeans, unfamiliar with the vagaries of financing real estate in Manhattan believed that Trump was a major player in that world. Trump, however is from Queens County, which is like being from Topeka as far as the guys who build in Manhattan are concerned. Brooklyn in those days was still a waste-land, the Bronx a slum, Queens confusing and no one ever wanted to invest a dollar in Staten Island. The people who actually own Manhattan are the Rudins, the Dursts, S.L. Green, Tishman-Spyer, Steven Roth, the Milstein's and about a dozen other primarily Jewish families, and," Kavanagh emphasized, "they were not going to do business with a German bank."

Victoria absorbed what Kavanagh had to say. "The fact that Deutsche has been in legal trouble for many years because of its affiliation with Trump shows it's true, whatever Trump touches, dies."

The next day Kavanagh was on an American Airlines flight to Memphis with a stopover for an hour in Chicago. Arriving in Memphis, he took a taxi to the Holiday Inn on Union Avenue in the downtown section of the city. Ava had called the hotel to say that Kavanagh would pick up Ray's suitcase. The front desk manager brought the suitcase from the storage room and turned it over to Kavanagh who signed a receipt for the duffel type travel bag. He had a reservation at the Hilton Garden Inn, which also was on Union Avenue three blocks away. He walked the three blocks pulling his rolling suitcase and carrying Ray's duffel.

Kavanagh checked in at the Hilton Garden Inn, mysteriously named because there wasn't a garden on the premises. He preferred Hilton hotels since reading an article in *Forbes* a while back naming the Hilton organization America's best employer. Hilton didn't offer unlimited snack foods and an adult playground environment to its employees. Instead the hotel company consciously supported and encouraged staff members and paid above the industry standard while offering comprehensive health benefits.

Once in his room on the top floor, Kavanagh open Ray's duffel spreading out its contents on the bed. What he found was unremarkable. Underwear and socks for four days, a clean pair of jeans, three shirts in laundry wrapping, a pair of black Sketchers and sleep wear. Ray's shaving kit contained what any man would use while traveling. Kavanagh was about to replace everything in the bag when he found an iPod in a side compartment. Upon opening the iPod, he saw a claim check from a public parking facility near the Holiday Inn. Written on the cardboard claim check was **GMC.** Now we're getting somewhere, Kavanagh thought.

He left the hotel retracing his steps toward the Holiday Inn. Across Union Avenue was the municipal parking garage. Kavanagh was armed with the truck's keys, a copy of the truck's registration and the claim check. He anticipated having a problem securing the truck since it had been about two months since Ray left it at the garage. He handed the claim check to the attendant, a young man, situated in a small office behind thick window glass with a small opening at the bottom. Kavanagh was about to begin to argue that he had the right to pick up the truck when the attendant asked for the parking fee, $472. Kavanagh pushed a credit card through the opening, holding his breath until the attendant returned the claim check marked paid along with a receipt for the credit card transaction.

Two or three minutes passed until the black GMC Sierra appeared from somewhere in the garage. It seemed to be enormous to Kavanagh who growing up in Manhattan didn't have a driver's license until his third year in college. He had never driven a truck and felt intimidated by the sheer size of the vehicle, which appeared dragon-like as if fire would roar from the headlights. With some difficulty he pulled himself up and into the driver's seat. It was as if he entered an airplane's cockpit. Lights and dials were all over the dashboard surrounding a GPS screen. He adjusted the power seat, which had a dozen positions. The truck's seats were leather, and a BOSE sound system filled the space with music at the perfect pitch.

Kavanagh eased the truck out of the garage and onto Union Avenue toward Beale Street. He had to drive around the block where his hotel was situated so he could enter the parking lot by making a simple right turn without turning against on-coming traffic. Once in the lot he found a space away from the street, locked the truck and vowed to himself that he would not drive it again. He had noticed that the truck's GPS had flashed a message as soon as he put the truck in gear at the parking garage. It said, "34 minutes to 1536 Evadne Avenue. Traffic is light."

Feeling pretty good after finding the truck, Kavanagh left the hotel and headed toward Beale Street, the city's iconic center for music. Once he was in the center of the barbeque and blues district he looked for a place to have lunch. Not surprising, most of the bars that featured live music were only open at night. None of the cafes that served lunch appealed to him, so Kavanagh asked the two police officers patrolling Beale Street where was the best place for lunch. Surprisingly, they emphatically recommended the Majestic Grill located not on Beale Street but a few blocks away on South Main. In ten minutes, Kavanagh found the Majestic Grill that was located in a former silent movie theater opened originally in 1913. The old theater's Beaux Arts décor was still in place creating the atmosphere of another time for the restaurant.

While waiting to be seated, Kavanagh checked his phone and read headlines from *The New York Times* proclaiming, that a relative of Donald Trump was killed by a city bus on New York's Fifth Avenue and the jackal that had taken over Rush Limbaugh's calculated radio lies was found dead from an apparent suicide. The reports made Kavanagh wonder if in fact Limbaugh really died from cancer or had he been slowly poisoned.

After wrestling with menu choices, Kavanagh ordered Memphis BBQ Nachos and the Crispy Chicken sandwich garnished with pickled cucumber and onion salad on a sweet role and parmesan potato fries. He drank a made-in-Memphis Fireside Amber Ale, which he enjoyed enough to have another. And he called Ava to tell her that he had Ray's clothing and found his truck. She thanked him without much enthusiasm and said her brother would go to Memphis tomorrow and pick it up. She was letting Don have the truck since she had no use for it. Kavanagh told Ava that Don can pick up the key at the front desk of the Hilton Garden Inn as he was returning to New York as soon as he could book a flight. He would send the other truck key back to Ava by FedEx. He also said that he would submit a list of his expenses to Ava for his trip to Memphis. Then he made one more call to Victoria Hope to check in and bring her up to date.

As he was drinking coffee at the meal's end, his iPhone beeped and a text from Sasha said, *"Did you forget me again?"* Kavanagh immediately called her. "I'm in Memphis. I'll explain when I see you. I'm going home tomorrow. Will you come to New York?" Sasha said she would call tonight to make plans for her visit to the east coast. He had one more task to accomplish in Memphis and left the Majestic Grill to pick up the car he rented for a day from Enterprise.

CHAPTER 26

Rayburn Office Building, Washington, DC

Since their single dinner together, Benni Zaiter had tried without much success to remain in contact with Lydia Merriman. He sent her flowers, invited Lydia to a musical at the Kennedy Center, sent notes and emails, but no texts since he didn't know her cell phone number. Because of his unusual attention, Lydia had asked one of her Washington staff members Tammy Brightwater, an attorney, to find out everything about Benni Zaiter and his company Amerind Botanical. Brightwater went to work engaging the best online and in person investigative techniques.

The first page of Brightwater's report listed her sources for the information that was gathered and presented to Lydia. The confidential investigation firm Harry Samuel Smith had been engaged to gather information. Sources included: a public records survey, a background and credit check, criminal records, a dark web search, marriage and ancestry records, social media search and a review of relevant news media.

A summary of the material presented provided Lydia with a focused picture of Zaiter and his company. He was born in 1972 near Bedminster, New Jersey. His father Armand, a Lebanese-American was an executive with Exxon. His entire career in the international oil business had been with Exxon from the time when the company was called Esso. Benni's mother was a member of the horsey set that lived around Bedminster. When Benni was five years old, the family moved to Beirut, Lebanon when Armand was appointed the chief of Middle East operations for the Exxon Corporation. Benni attended Catholic elementary and high schools, and graduated from the American University of Beirut.

Upon his graduation from the American University, Benni and his parents returned to the United States. Armand left Exxon and became a senior fellow with the American Petroleum Institute a Washington based trade association that serves as the main lobbying group for the oil and natural gas industry. Benni, due to his fluidity in Arabic, French, and English began a position with the American Association of Exporters and Importers (AAEI). He stayed with the trade organization for fourteen years, moving up in its executive ranks while making contacts in the European Union, Africa, India, and Turkey. He becomes the president and CEO in 2008 of Marigold Mineral & Chemical Corporation, based in Charleston, South Carolina. The company declared Chapter 7 bankruptcy in 2013. Benni Zaiter was ousted amid charges of embezzlement and incompetency.

Zaiter relocated to Santa Barbara, California and leased an impressive home in the Mission Valley section. He attracted financial backers and produced several motion pictures that were financially successful in the international market, but were not distributed in this country. He was married twice, once for seven years and one for two years resulting in divorces. There are no children from the marriages. After a series of lessor films, all financial disasters, Zaiter left the motion picture business and California. Through former contacts, Zaiter secured a position with the International Chamber of Commerce. He worked in the Chamber's program encouraging the sale of tobacco products especially cigarettes in third world countries. He was successful in spreading the poison associated with smoking, and the levels of cancer and heart disease related to smoking rose in the places (Russia, Africa, and India) where adequate health care was missing.

Finally, in 2022, Zaiter joined the newly created company Amerind Botanical as the CEO. Amerind was defined as "Native American." The company's mission is the development of pharmaceutical manufacturing in the United States to replace all of that kind of production going on in India. He promised to attract major financial investment from Wall Street bankers and hedge fund managers. However, investments so far in Amerind Botanical had not come from traditional financial organizations, but from Russian nationals living in ultra-luxury condominiums in Manhattan. Since the company wasn't publicly traded, its financials were not open for inspection. However, after extensive investigation, it was determined that only a fraction of the investment required for acquiring the site and building the research and manufacturing facility has been committed. However, further investigation uncovered some interest in Amerind from Goldman Sachs, Blackstone Group, Brookfield Asset Management, Carlyle Group, and Apollo Global, but to date none have made offers or committed funds.

Lydia absorbed the material that painted a less than flattering picture of Benni Zaiter's company and his personal background. The narrative continued with the real estate report. A two-hundred-acre tract of land situated east of Poughkeepsie, NY had been optioned for $50,000 by Amerind Botanical Corporation. The site is for the company's proposed pharmaceutical research and manufacturing center. The purchase price of the site is over three million dollars. Several billboards measuring 30' by 12' erected on the site proclaimed the establishment of the Amerind facility. At 55 Main Street in the center of Poughkeepsie's central business district, Amerind Botanical leased a four-story historic building to serve as its headquarters while the proposed research and manufacturing facility is built. The Main Street property would also serve as the marketing arm of the company, establishing distribution channels for the new source of medications, which is the underpinning of the company.

Benni Zaiter's personal financial information followed. A TransUnion credit report showed fourteen active credit cards in

Benni Zaiter's name with a total balance of $81,232. A three month analysis of Zaiter's credit use showed only minimum required payments made on most credit cards, which resulted in an up to 24% increase in debt annually.

Zaiter, the report continued lived in Spackenkill, in Dutchess County, NY in a four bedroom, four bath home built in 1979 by the architect Roy Sigvard Johnson in the style of Frank Lloyd Wright. The 4,244 square foot home featured redwood siding, but has primarily exterior glass walls. The home, situated on four acres, had mountain views, an in-ground pool and a two car garage. It was valued at $1,100,000. The property is leased to Zaiter at $5,700 per month on a three year lease that began six months ago. The rest of the report contained sources for the information provided, copies of news stories regarding Zaiter and his various businesses, all on-line listings related to him and an analysis done by McKinsey & Company regarding the amount of investment and infrastructure required in order to enter global pharmaceutical production in the United States.

My lord, Lydia thought, was there any truth to anything Benni Zaiter said? The report was edifying. Compliments to Tammy Brightwater, the author. Now she certainly didn't want to attend the reception scheduled at Zaiter's home the following Thursday evening, but New York's governor had personally asked Lydia to be there. Apparently some of the people from the major investment firms would be attending, along with the lieutenant governor and the speaker of the state assembly. It was something Lydia had to do even though she had grave misgivings being associated with Benni and his project.

CHAPTER 27

Memphis Blues

Kavanagh wasn't a risk taker when it came to physical situations. He didn't ski, sky dive or scuba. He wrote tough letters to editors, sent out bundles of emails supporting or denouncing politicians and spent his teaching career strongly advocating for social justice. Now he was putting his health and safety on the line by driving to South Memphis, the old industrial section about a half hour from downtown. Ray's truck GPS had automatically brought up the address, 1536 Evadne Avenue, and Kavanagh suspected it was the place Ray frequented when he was in Memphis.

The building Kavanagh drove past on Evadne Avenue was a single-story industrial structure containing about four thousand square feet. It was secured by an eight-foot-high chain-link fence that surrounded an open space in the building's front. The fence was lined with white plywood and topped off with concertina wire. Kavanagh didn't see any other place to enter the building except through the gate in the fence. The building's few windows were boarded over. A cell tower that reached up about one hundred and fifty feet stood alongside of the structure and was also surrounded by fencing at its base. The tower had three dishes at its top. No doubt the building's occupants had instant cell phone connection to anyone anywhere.

Kavanagh drove by only twice because he guessed that the street was constantly swept by cameras. The building was located less than a half mile from the access road to Interstate 240, an auxiliary highway leading to Interstate 40, a major east-west road running through the center of the country. Kavanagh stopped at a Pilot truck stop near the entrance ramp to I-240. He parked at the side of the truck stop's food store and bought a bottle of diet Coke. Asking himself, what he was doing, Kavanagh walked back toward the building on Evadne Avenue. He watched two vehicles about fifteen minutes apart drive into the fenced in area after the gates opened automatically. He didn't see the car's occupants and from where he was stationed behind a utility company's shed, he hoped he wasn't seen.

Without being certain, because he had no real evidence, Kavanagh believed he had found the place Ray reported to when he came to Memphis for an assignment. Kavanagh suspected Ray had been an operative for the people who were eliminating the dangerous individuals working against the nation's core values, but who are they? However, trying to stay out of sight on a street in South Memphis made Kavanagh realize that his quest to find out any more about Ray and the people he worked for was over. Still not really sure why he became involved in the first place, and how, he asked himself, could Lydia Merriman possibly be part of a series of murders? Of course not. It was impossible. Answering his own question, Kavanagh knew it was time to go home.

Indeed, as Kavanagh had suspected, the white building was the operations center for the un-named deadly team that carried out the directives from the Knox group. The structure contained a large storeroom with shelves holding the latest in electronic surveillance equipment, large quantities of military grade armament, packages of surgeons' gloves, boxes of single use cell phones, night vision goggles and dozens of cartons of different brands of power bars and energy drinks. A sound proof planning room had been built in the center of the space and a modern restroom complex with shower stalls had been installed. Three small offices with glass fronts lined one wall along with a compact kitchen. The rest of the interior had been finished with wallboard over the original cinderblocks. Bright colors and artwork adorned the walls creating a carpeted executive-level office atmosphere.

Ray had been recruited for work with this group by a man he had met at the gun range he frequented outside of St. Louis. Eddy Burke was an ordinary-appearing man. Just under six feet tall, hair cut short, clean shaven and neatly dressed in flannel shirts and khaki slacks. He was a crack shot, and Ray commented on Eddy's ability to always hit the bull's eye on the paper target. Eddy having watched Ray's use of weapons was equally impressed by his accuracy.

After shooting at targets on a Saturday afternoon, Ray and Eddy left the range and walked to nearby Clancy Brother's Bar for beers and pizzas. The cold Budweiser, a St. Louis icon, along with pizza not quite as good as Domino's, help create a friendship between the two men. Eddy admitted he had worked for the State Department in some of the world's hotspots. When Ray inquired about the kind of work Eddy had done, Eddy just said, "Whatever was needed." Leaving Ray to imagine he was in the company of a black opps agent and frankly was intrigued by the world that Eddy represented. Was he still involved? Ray wondered about that.

Two weeks later, Ray and Eddy were at the same bar after their shooting sessions. Eddy asked, "Ray, how did you get to be such a good marksman? Were you in the service?" Ray admitted that he had served two hitches in the Middle East, not as a combat soldier, but a truck mechanic. He explained that he practiced with firearms as often as he could, and won sharp shooter medals. He said he missed not seeing any action. He wasn't afraid of combat and believed that he would have been a good fighter.

Two months went by and Ray and Eddy had gotten together four times at Clancy Brother's. This time, Eddy led the conversation. He pointedly asked, "Ray are you interested in doing something else, not fixing motors? Do you want to make a lot of money and have the kind of adventures you missed out in Afghanistan?"

"Sure, but I'm married now. We have two young children, twins. I can't be away for long periods of time." Ray had assumed the offer was for a job as a mercenary, a soldier of fortune, a Blackwater hired gunman earning $900 a day in Africa or South America or Saudi Arabia. "I guess I'm not really interested, but why are you telling me about this job? Who do you work for?"

Eddy hesitated before speaking. He was evaluating Ray again before exposing any more to him. "I'm loosely affiliated with an ultra-secret agency that has a special task. It involves dealing with the people who are trying to hurt our country by supporting a fascist controlled society." Ray's quizzical look made it obvious he didn't understand what Eddy said. "Look, I can't say any more unless you really want to get involved. I can say that it doesn't involve being away from home for more than three or four days at a time."

"That's a different story," Ray said. "Tell me more about all that."

"Ray, do you know about the Sons of Liberty and what they did prior to the American Revolution?" Ray appeared even more confused. "Okay," Eddy continued. "The Sons of Liberty was a secret organizations of patriots that fought against the British control of parts of everyday life in Colonial America. For instance the heavy tax on tea. They would be called guerilla fighters today. Some of the success of the Revolution was due to the Sons of Liberty. They sabotaged the British army and assassinated tax collectors and other British officials."

"Then," Eddy Burke continued. "There was John Brown's raid on the Harpers Ferry arsenal in Virginia. John Brown led a small force to capture armament for a slave rebellion. It was another example in our history of a secret group trying to make it better for everyone. It was the spark that ignited the Civil War. They did what the government couldn't do." Ray absorbed the history, but said nothing. "Look Ray," Eddy picked up the conversation, I've had my eye on you for a while. You're an expert marksman, and to tell the truth, I looked at your Army record. You moved up to corporal quickly and if you stayed in would have made sergeant as soon as reenlisting. Your record is excellent, not one black mark. Your closest buddy, Paul Santos, now a staff sergeant at Fort Bliss in Texas said you were the most dependable man he has ever known."

Ray was astonished. "How did you get my army file? How did you find Paul Santos?" He stopped to think. "Okay I get it. You guys are CIA or something like that. Am I right?"

Eddy smiled, "It doesn't make any difference who we are. Just realize that we have the ability to carry out important strikes against enemies of our country. It's important what we will do. The nation will be stronger and you can be part of it. And by the way, be paid more than you ever imagined."

"Jesus, I don't know," was Ray's response. "Is all this legal?"

"Ray, legal is a term that applies to everyday activities. Bank robbers, muggers, dope dealers are acting illegally. When government acts in a manner that's necessary to protect its citizens, even though it may be off the usual path of behavior, sometimes we must allow for that kind of deviation." He gave Ray a card with only a phone number written on it. "Take a day or two. Think about what I said. Don't say anything to anyone, even your wife. If I don't hear from you by Monday, I'll assume you aren't interested. Also, we won't see each other again. After Monday, Eddy Burke won't exist."

Ray didn't wait for Monday. He called the number on the card Sunday night. He made the decision to work with Eddy's people because he didn't want to spend the rest of his working life repairing motors at an hourly wage. Of course, the Eddy he thought he knew, thought was a friend, didn't actually exist. Who the hell was Eddy, Ray kept asking himself? The voice answering the call gave Ray instructions. He must give his boss at the Caterpillar dealership two weeks' notice that he was leaving. No sudden moves. He should tell Ava that he had applied and had been accepted to the structural steel workers union, and his specialty after some training, due to his Mohawk heritage on his mother's side, will be the setting of the last high beams on skyscraper buildings. Ray was given an address in Memphis. An industrial building on the south side of the city where he'll meet Eddy's people. He'll be paid $20,000 in advance when he arrives at the building with the chain-link fence and concertina wire at the top.

The drive to Memphis from St. Louis took four-and-a-half hours to cover the two hundred and eighty-three miles along highway U.S. 55. Ray left before dawn on Monday and found 1536 Evadne Avenue without any trouble. As he pulled his ten-year old Ford truck up to the gates at the building's front, they opened and he drove into the small courtyard. Expecting an armed security guard, Ray was surprised when the man greeting him looked like a teacher. He wore a blue button down shirt, khaki slacks, and Sperry Top Sider boat shoes. The man, introducing himself as Jack Coen was tall and lean and gray-haired. Ray suspected that Jack Coen like Eddy Burke would not be known anywhere else.

They talked for a long time in the sound proof room. Coen spoke of the great mission they were embarking upon. The chance to right the most pressing wrongs of a society that had allowed the most terrible elements to exert control of its government and the other social institutions, where children had mimicked the nation's president in expressing hate for anyone with differences, where a major television network had turned millions into non-thinking bigots and encouraged ignorance among a large percent of the population, where the Republican Party gave up its tradi-tional role and enabled the growth of the greatest threat to consti-tutional government in the nation's history.

"Ray," Jack Coen sounding like a professor, went on. "Let's talk about the ARA. At one time it was a club for sportsmen and target shooters like yourself. But over the years it became a dangerous political organization dedicated to selling armament around the world. It bought congressmen and senators, governors and who knows who else. There are creditable people who have claimed the enormous amount contributed to Bernie Sanders' cam-paign in February 2020, about $48 million, was primarily Russian money funneled through the ARA. They wanted Bernie to be the

Democrat's candidate because he would have been easy to defeat in the general election. I guess we'll never know the truth, but something has to be done about the ARA." That was Ray's orientation to the work he choose, which he became skilled at doing until it killed him.

CHAPTER 28

Lydia's Dilemma

It was Thursday and Lydia had promised to attend the investor's reception at Benni Zaiter's home, but she had second thoughts about even being in Zaiter's presence. She had come back to her district from Washington early that day because the Governor had called personally requesting her presence at the event. Along with Lydia, a star-studded cast of state and local politicians were invited. Most were more interested in the lavish buffet and open bar than the introduction of Amerind Botanica to the local community and Wall Street bankers. Representatives of New York's medical community also were expected to attend along with the leadership of the county's colleges and universities.

Lydia regretted that she was attending the reception alone. Frankly she missed Kavanagh's steady presence and guidance. She hadn't replaced Kavanagh since he left her staff to promote his book. There wasn't anyone on her district staff who she wanted to attend with her, and therefore she was on her own. Right now she was focused on what she would wear tonight. After pulling out a half dozen dresses from her room size closet, Lydia settled for a navy blue straight wool and silk blend dress worn with pearls and a Hermes scarf.

The invitation called for appearances at 7:00 pm so Lydia left her home at 6:45 for the forty-five minute drive to Zaiter's home.

There was valet parking, and the local police were helping with traffic control on the narrow road leading to the brightly lit glass front house. Lydia was mildly surprise by the larger crowd than she had expected. Once relinquishing her car to the parking attendant, Lydia entered the house and estimated that about one hundred guests were there. The Lieutenant Governor and the County Executive were together and welcomed Lydia to the gathering. Both of them were featured speakers, and Lydia was expected to sum up the presentations and answer questions regarding the federal support for the project.

Benni Zaiter seemed relieved to see Lydia. "I was worried that you were not coming here tonight," he ventured. I just had a that feeling since we hadn't spoken since our dinner date."

"Benni, it was not a dinner date. You know better." Lydia had avoided Benni's attempts to contact her since the first time he came to her office in the Rayburn Office Building. She had agreed to meet him for dinner later that evening because she didn't feel like being on her own that day. However it was a mistake to allow Benni any time with her as he took advantage of the situation. Twice he sent flowers to her at her office, and made endless attempts to speak with her on the phone or in person. After absorbing the material on Benni Zaiter put together by her staffer, Lydia wanted to distance herself from him, but because of local political realities, she couldn't do that right now.

Lydia moved around the spacious home. There were tables throughout the main floor with servers offering a wide selection of spectacular food. Large bowls of chipped ice held giant shrimp, Wellfleet oysters and clams on the half shell. Two chefs were busy producing sushi and sashimi of every variety. A carving station offered turkey, brisket and roast beef on rolls from Manhattan's Sullivan Street Bakery. Another served tiny bagels from Murry's on Sixth Avenue covered with paper thin sliced smoked Nova Scotia salmon from Russ & Daughters on Houston Street, and a chef resembling Emeril Lagasse filled bowls with New Orleans style Etouffee. Bar tenders pouring champagne and any other drink desired were everywhere. Clearly Benni Zaiter intended to impress everyone who was there.

At 9 o'clock chimes sounded and Zaiter standing next to the grand piano spoke into the wireless microphone he was holding. "Good evening everyone. If I haven't had the pleasure to talk with you tonight, I apologize and will make it up to you anytime you're available." He went on to give an overview of Amerind Botanical and its future as the major manufacturer of pharmaceuticals that brought back that industry to the United States. He introduced the company's director of research, an eminent scientist, and the physician who was the company's board chairman a leader in bio-medical investing. Both men spoke about the obvious need to bring back the manufacturing of medicines to our country.

Benni Zaiter followed up by unveiling a large rendering of the Amerind Botanical's campus soon to be constructed a short distance east of Poughkeepsie. There were appreciative comments made by audience members especially the group of county officials. The Lieutenant Governor, a woman from north western New York near Buffalo, spoke for ten minutes outlining the support the state will provide in the form of tax abatements, credits for creating new jobs and access roads to the new corporate site. Her enthusiasm was infectious and she received a round of applause. Next there were short statements of support from the County Executive and Poughkeepsie's mayor.

Zaiter, beaming from the positive reception of the speakers took the microphone back and introduced Lydia as the federal government's representative to the Amerind Botanica project, who would work on legislation to prohibit the production in India of medicine for Americans. She was appalled by his statement, and made her way to the room's front frowning. Lydia had to toss out her prepared remarks in order to rebut Zaiter's statement. "I'm pleased to see all of you tonight. The development of new business projects in the Hudson Valley is a priority for the Governor's office, and the commitment made to Amerind as outlined by the

Lieutenant Governor moments ago is an important sign of the support that New York State and Dutchess County will provide."

She hesitated before going on. "However, I have to clarify some of the statements made tonight. I do not represent the federal government. This is my congressional district so, of course, I will support all businesses especially those that have indicated their plan to hire five hundred new people to jobs on all levels. However, I am not involved with any proposed legislation to prohibit pharmaceutical manufacturing abroad." She deliberately left out the India issue. "I want to emphasize again that I don't represent the House of Representatives or the White House." I wish the best of luck to Mr. Zaiter and Amerind Botanical's leadership, and I welcome them to our beautiful Hudson Valley." She left the microphone on the piano and began to walk toward the coat check area on her way to leaving.

Lydia was almost immediately surrounded by some of the Wall Street people and news media representatives. "Congresswoman Merriman." The *Wall Street Journal* reporter was the first to ask what was on the minds of everyone in the group around Lydia. "So as far as you know, nothing is going on in Washington to bring back pharmaceutical manufacturing?"

"No, I didn't say that. There may be some of that going on, but I'm not involved and therefore I can't comment, but if that was happening, I would certainly support it."

The reporter came back with another question. "Haven't you been brought up to date by Mr. Zaiter?"

"I met Mr. Zaiter only once. I don't know that much about the project."

"Really?" The reporter continued. "Your office hired Harry Samuel Smith to investigate Benni Zaiter and McKinsey & Company to determine if the actual concept of bringing back off shore pharmaceutical manufacturing was logical. You had dinner with Mr. Zaiter. What did you talk about?" Lydia ignored the *Wall Street Journal's* reporter and turned to a young woman standing nearby.

"Congresswoman, I'm Sally Dolan from Goldman Sachs. The financial community was told that Washington was poised to pass legislation to phase out the foreign manufacturing of pharmaceuticals. Are we ready to take over that much production?"

Lydia remained outwardly calm, but was raging inside. "I don't know. Pharmaceutical manufacturing will be new to our area. I'm going to have to catch up. I can't say anymore." The Albany reporter of *The New York Times,* an acquaintance of Lydia whispered to her, "What the hell is going on?"

Her answer, also whispered was, "I wish I knew." She had to find Benni Zaiter who was saying good night to guests. He indicated she should wait in the library and would join her soon.

Lydia found Zaiter's library in the back of the house. The room was large with a high ceiling and had book shelves covering three walls. However the number of books on the shelves was limited to a few dozen. A long leather sofa dominated the room's center with a narrow glass coffee table almost as long as the sofa. A desk was situated in one corner with two desk top computers and a laser printer on its surface. The room's windows were covered with dark shades and the only light came from a round studded glass Turkish fixture hanging from the ceiling in the room's center. Lydia brought out her cell phone and called Grace Ellen her chief of staff in Washington.

Lydia was livid with anger. "Grace Ellen, I was asked tonight by a *Wall Street Journal* reporter about our engaging Harry Samuel Smith and McKinsey to investigate Benni Zaiter." She hesitated before going on to catch her breath. "The worst part is I was also asked about having dinner with him. Why did that happen? Who in our office is talking about these things? I'm a little insane right now so don't take it personally. I need you to fix this."

Grace Ellen who was almost worshipful in her loyalty to Lydia was crushed. "Oh my God. How did that happen? I am so sorry. I'll get to the bottom of this, I promise." She was already planning to ferret out the identity of the staff member who leaked to the *Journal,* and fire whoever it was, immediately.

CHAPTER 29

Lydia's Crisis

Lydia's phone was about to die. "Grace Ellen, I'll talk with you in the morning. Don't worry. We can deal with this. I just had to talk with you to focus on what to do. Go to bed. I'm sorry I dropped all this on you so late at night." They said goodbye planning to talk for a long time the next day.

As Lydia zipped the iPhone into her purse with a shoulder strap that she wore for all receptions, the library's door flew open and Benni Zaiter burst into the room. "You god damned bitch. How dare you investigate me? I've been telling reporters just now that you're crazy, paranoid, unfit for office."

Lydia was shocked by Zaiter's venom, and knew she had to leave right away, but he blocked her way. As she attempted to walk past Zaiter, he swung blindly striking Lydia's face hard enough to knock her to the floor. As she attempted to get up, Zaiter hit her again this time with his fist.

Lydia fell back again, but landed against the glass table shattering it and causing multiple injuries. Zaiter seemed to have disappeared. He'd turned off the room's one overhead light. Now in the pitch dark room Lydia hurt and bleeding pulled herself up unsure what to do. Trying to avoid the jagged glass, she maneuvered away from the leather sofa, but tripped on something in her way causing her to fall against the desk and then to the floor again.

Trying not to panic, Lydia knew she was in grave danger of dying. She felt her own blood everywhere and her right arm and left leg were not helping her get up and out of the dark room. Somehow she was able to rise again. Now in agony she grabbed on to the desk chair, which didn't support her, but rolled away on the hardwood floor causing Lydia to fall again losing consciousness.

At some point Zaiter returned to the library and when he turned on the light saw Lydia bleeding and unconscious. Somehow he was surprised even though he had assaulted her. Zaiter quickly left and yelled to his assistant, "Matt, Matt where the hell are you? I need you right now." A confused Matt Hanson ran across the house to where Zaiter was standing and yelling.

"What happened here?" Matt was panicked seeing Lydia torn up and bleeding maybe dying in front of them.

"Never mind about that. Get her coat and wrap her in it. I don't want her blood all over my house." Matt rushed to the coat racks in the foyer returning with Lydia's long black coat. "Okay, now get her car. You'll drive her to the hospital in Poughkeepsie, Vassar Brothers. I'll follow in my car."

With her Jeep in front of the house, Matt carried Lydia out of the house and placed her across the back seat fastening a seat belt around her. Zaiter had said to go to the emergency department's entrance and leave Lydia in the Jeep with the warning lights flashing and alarm sounding. Zaiter stayed in his car far enough from Vassar Brothers Hospital so that he and Matt could get away quickly without being seen.

An emergency medical technician checked the vehicle left in front of the emergency department with its lights flashing and alarm blasting. He found Lydia moaning and summoned the emergency department staff. As soon as Lydia was lifted onto a rolling stretcher, IVs were started and she was surrounded by nurses and doctors. The director of emergency services of Vassar Brothers Medical Center was Dr. Michele Espinoza and she took over ordering scans, x-rays and a blood transfusion. After cutting away Lydia's clothing and carefully examining her, she put out calls for an orthopedic surgeon to assess Lydia's arm and leg injuries, a general surgeon to access the deep contusions covering Lydia's body, and an oral surgeon for the damage to her face. The doctor introduced medicine into the IV to relieve pain and allow Lydia to sleep until morning.

Early the following day, a groggy Lydia Merriman painfully looked around trying to understand where she was and what had happened to her. Was it a nightmare? Had she imagined being assaulted by Benni Zaiter? Why can't she move her arms and legs? She began to scream, and in a moment a nurse moved from the next ICU enclosure to Lydia's side. "Hello, I know you can speak because you can yell. We don't know your name or what happened to you. Are you in pain? I suspect you are and I'll help with that. I have to call Dr. Espinosa now that you're awake. Who assaulted you, and were you raped? We have to report this to the police."

Lydia was panicked. She tried to answer the nurse's questions, but gave up and closed her eyes. Apparently a new drug had been introduced into her IV because she returned to a twilight state not caring about anything even her critical condition. She dreamed about early and better times at Turner Television and about her son as a young boy. When she awoke two hours later she was crying. Sitting nearby was a young woman wearing a doctor's white coat. "Can you speak to me?" Lydia nodded. The doctor continued. The chief of medicine examined you after I did last night. Your tests show kidney damage, a fractured radius of your right arm, broken bones in your wrist, and fractured tibia of your left leg. That's why you're in restraints. We're going to repair both limbs today, which will relieve most of your pain. You have deep contusions and lacerations all over, but they were treated last night by excellent trauma surgeries. Your face has breaks under the skin especially around your left eye. An oral surgeon from NYU specializing in maxillofacial surgery has read your x-rays and will see you tomorrow.

Lydia summoned up her strength and said, "Doctor, thank you."

"That's why we're here. By the way, I'm Michele Espinoza, and I know who you are. I sent a security guy to move your car and to look for your handbag. He almost missed it because it's small, but it was under the seat in back. I voted for you. So Congresswoman Lydia Merriman why are you my patient?"

Lydia found she could only slowly answer the doctor's question. "Please doctor, don't let anyone know I'm here." Lydia had to gather her thoughts, "I was at an event and was attacked by a mad-man. I fell onto a glass table which shattered. After that I don't know anything. How did I get here?"

"I don't know. What I do know is that if you had been allowed to hemorrhage any longer you would have died. That was criminal negligence on top of assault, maybe attempted murder. I should call the police." Lydia eyes showed panic and she made the doctor know that she wanted to keep her situation a secret. "All right, I understand, no one will know you're here at least for a while. I'm admitting you as Jane Roe, but your medical insurance may expose that you are here."

Lydia actually smiled a little and painfully said in a low voice. "Please find my wallet. It's in my purse." The doctor had Lydia's wallet on the table behind her. That's how she knew Lydia's identity. She put the wallet close to Lydia on the bed. Lydia using her left hand awkwardly fished out some plastic cards. She looked carefully and handed one to the doctor. "Use this to pay the charges here. It's in my son's name. I was going to send it to him today. He's using his father's last name now so my being here will be kept a secret." The black American Express card had a $50,000 limit. The effort exhausted Lydia and her eyes closed.

"All right. I want you to rest until surgery this afternoon. Limited fluids only right now. The anesthesiologist will be in to see you later. Oh, and by the way, some good news, you were not sexually assaulted. Your dress was torn down the front, but your underwear was intact and there's no indication of any sexual contact. I'll see you after your surgery. Don't worry you're in really good hands." They smiled at each other and Lydia exhausted from the effort she had made with the doctor fell back to sleep.

The two surgeries took place simultaneously. The orthopedic surgeons and surgical nurses completed their tasks perfectly and returned Lydia to post-op for recovery from the anesthesia. She stayed in post-op for only a day, received two more blood transfusions and was transferred back to a private room. The next afternoon the oral surgeon showed up and lightly touched the socket around Lydia's left eye. "I can feel the fractures. Your eye socket has to be repaired otherwise your vision will be affected." He looked at the x-rays mounted on a light box on the wall. "I want to try something before we talk about surgery, Okay?" Lydia tired and confused just nodded.

The oral surgeon, his name was Dr. Small, raised the head of Lydia's bed to a sitting position. He put on surgical gloves and asked Lydia to open her mouth wide. He slipped his hand with index finger extended over her teeth and up under her facial skin close to her eye. He carefully manipulated the small fractures into their proper places. Upon withdrawing his hand after the procedure, which took only a few seconds he said, "That's it. You'll be fine. When you get out of here you can come to see me for a panoramic x-ray. They don't have one here." He smiled and said goodbye to a happier Lydia.

Dr. Espinoza spent more time with Lydia than with other patients. She usually took her lunch break in Lydia's room. They were becoming friends. "Lydia we'll be throwing you out of here in three days if your blood work continues to improve. You'll need help with everything so our social worker is coming to see you regarding transferring to a rehabilitation center." The doctor waited for Lydia's reaction. When she didn't react Dr. Espinoza looking pained said, "I've left alone the main issue until now. Why you are here. You were assaulted, attacked and practically left for dead. You know your assailant. What are you going to do about him? I want to file a police report. If you were a man instead of a woman, your attacker would be in jail."

"Michele I can never thank you sufficiently for saving my life. We can't file a police report. The right wing media will make a circus out of my story. I'll end up the cause rather than the victim. I'll be assaulted again on the internet." She knew that the gross hatred by the cowards who flood social media with lies had not stopped since Trump. If anything they're worse because they're scattered without a potential dictator in the White House. Painfully she looked at the doctor. "They hate women like you and me." She hesitated before going on. "And I'm not going to a nursing home. I want to go home. I'll figure it out."

Lydia hadn't considered being anywhere else. She had adjusted to Vassar Brothers Hospital and the skill and kindness of its staff. As soon as she was able to text she had contacted Grace Ellen explaining that she had flu and felt terrible, and was not to be disturbed for a while. Congress was out on recess so it was a down time anyway. She wasn't going to another health facility where her identity wouldn't be protected. She knew what she had to do. She had mastered using her iPhone with her left hand and touched the number she once called regularly. "Kavanagh, its Lydia. I'm in Vassar Brothers. Yes, the hospital. I need you. Room 5610. I'm not registered as a patient. I'll explain, just get here soon."

CHAPTER 30

Vassar Brothers Medical Center

When Kavanagh entered the hospital room he was shocked seeing Lydia in bed with her leg encased by a white cast, her arm in a blue sling and obvious injuries all over. "Jesus, Lydia what the hell happened to you?" Then he saw Michele Espinoza in a white coat and realized she was a doctor. "I'm sorry, Lydia. Doctor, I can come back later."

"No," Lydia called out. "Stay here. This is Dr. Espinoza, my good friend, who also happens to be the doctor who saved my life. Michele this is Kavanagh. It's a long story."

"Hello Kavanagh, I'm glad you're here. She," indicating Lydia, "requires lots of help once she leaves here. Can you do that for her?"

Without hesitation, Kavanagh said, "Of course. Now what the hell happened to her?" Lydia quietly told her story of the night at Benni Zaiter's home. As much as she remembered. The doctor filled in listing Lydia's injuries and the procedures she had undergone. Kavanagh took it all in, his complexion turning red. Clearly he was planning to hurt Zaiter, but that had already been seen to by Lydia on her own.

Just the day before, feeling stronger, Lydia asked Michele Espinoza to buy a single-use cell phone with a prepaid phone card for her. The doctor, believing that Lydia's iPhone was no longer working, offered her phone to Lydia. "Thank you, but please buy the other phone for me. Take my credit card. Walgreen's sells them. I have to make a confidential call. It's congressional business." Michele agreed and bought a phone for Lydia.

Having the cheap cell phone in her possession gave Lydia a sense of power for the first time since she almost lost her life. She was reminded of the night Carleton Ruiz came to her townhouse in Columbia Heights informing Lydia that she had to take his place as the Zodiac arranging for the murder of persons selected by the Knox group. What made the most impression on her was Ruiz's reporting that Steve Mellor's death, after being dropped from a helicopter, two hundred feet above a Manhattan street, was a three asterisk hit. And the death of the repulsive Alex Jones impaled alive on steel fence posts in the community he tortured was ordered by four asterisks.

Lydia using her left hand, carefully sent a text with the proper coding ordering the death of Benni Zaiter. After spelling his name, adding his address and position as CEO of Amerind Botanical, she hesitated just for a moment before tapping in five asterisks.

Kavanagh had arranged for his son Greg to pick up Lydia's Jeep from the hospital's parking lot and drive it to her home in Millbrook. Greg's girlfriend Tillie followed in her car. Eventually Kavanagh would bring it to a car wash that detailed car interiors to remove Lydia's blood from it. A call to the dean of nursing at Setoncliff University yielded names of nurses available to care for Lydia at home. He arranged to meet with the nurses the next day. Also a physical therapist was engaged for daily sessions. Kavanagh would have to figure a way to have meals served, but that had to wait a while so he went to the grocery store himself and stocked Lydia's refrigerator.

At Lydia's request Kavanagh took over communications between her office in Washington and the district. They worked out a tale of Lydia, after having flu, and feeling a little better went for a run. She became light headed and tripped over a curb sending her down into a concrete water run off culvert breaking her arm, wrist, and leg. She was at home recovering and receiving physical therapy. Lydia, really feeling a lot stronger, was able to speak regularly with Grace Ellen in Washington who was relieved that Kavanagh was back. But was he? They hadn't discussed anything except supporting Lydia until she was able to be a member of congress again. Oddly, Lydia was most concerned that the President be informed of her injuries from jogging, and that she will have a long rehabilitation. Kavanagh used all of his considerable talent to get that done, which resulted in Lydia receiving a hand written note from the President thanking her for service to the nation.

Now that Lydia had healed, she told her parents the falling while running story. They visited regularly coming from Queens in a car service arranged by Kavanagh. Lydia's tenant in Columbia Heights, the senator from Hawaii also visited Lydia in Millbrook twice.

Dr. Espinoza came to see Lydia at least once a week, twice accompanied by one of the orthopedic surgeons who had performed Lydia's surgery. Both of the doctors were satisfied with Lydia's progress and the hard casts on her arm and leg were removed and soft supports were substituted. Because Lydia's condition presumably resulting from a fall was now widely known, cards, email, flowers, fruit baskets, books, and other gifts poured into her home. Kavanagh had moved two staff people from Lydia's district office in Poughkeepsie to Millbrook to handle the volume of mail and deliveries. The flowers were sent to nursing homes and assisted living facilities, the fruit to Head Starts and other pre-schools, and the staff answered the cards and emails.

Kavanagh had essentially moved into a guest bedroom on the second floor of Lydia's home. Lydia's home office on the ground floor had been converted into her bedroom by adding a rented hospital bed. The room had an attached bathroom, so it was ideal for her. He often stayed late trying to catch up on the paper work so staying at the house made more sense than driving back to Peekskill. He spoke with Sasha as often as he could, just saying that Lydia had an accident and he was helping her until she was able to operate on her own again.

Sasha's reaction was half serious. "So you moved in with your girlfriend. How nice for you."

"You know very well that she was not my girlfriend, not that I didn't want her, I did, but that's water under the bridge, over the dam or wherever it goes. I'm not officially back on Lydia's staff, just helping out. I miss you but I can't get away from here for a while. Please be patient." They broke the connection after promising to talk daily. Kavanagh thinking about the conversation wondered if he and Sasha had just made some kind of commitment to each other.

A month went by and Lydia responded well to the daily hour of physical therapy. Her doctors released her as a patient and she began to make plans to return to Washington and her place in Columbia Heights. Lydia visited both of her district offices talking with the staffs and a few constituents representing organizations and other groups of supporters. She and Grace Ellen used Facetime everyday catching Lydia up on the issues that came to her congressional office from her committee assignments, the Speaker and the Democrats.

A week later, feeling a lot better she went back to work in Washington. Grace Ellen had prepared for Lydia's return by arranging a welcome back event in the Rayburn Reception Room. The Speaker and the entire New York congressional delegation attended along with many others Lydia served with on committees, along with some of members of the Black Congressional Caucus and several Senators. Kavanagh who had accompanied Lydia to Washington, had returned to New York as soon as Lydia was settled in under the watchful eyes of Grace Ellen.

He was in Millbrook packing up his belongings and cleaning up the bedroom he had used when Lydia called. "Why weren't you at my party today?" She sounded happy and he was relieved she had adjusted to being back in Washington again so quickly. "I expected you to be there. I was going to announce that you and I were working together again." He didn't say anything so Lydia continued. "Actually, I want to talk about something else. We were in the same house together for five weeks and I liked it. I know I wasn't the best company because I got tired a lot. But that was because of meds for pain and PT. I'm feeling a lot better and you have so much to do with that."

Kavanagh hadn't committed to working with Lydia again so he wondered where she was going. "Frankly Kavanagh, I want you to stay with me in Millbrook and here in Washington. I don't want to live alone anymore."

He was astounded. "Lydia, stay with you as what? What are you saying to me?

"As companions, maybe lovers. Where-ever it goes will be all right. We'll have to see. I liked having you around all the time. It was nice." Yes, he thought, because I managed the house, did the food shopping, dealt with staff and we watched Netflix together.

"You know Lydia, I can't count the times I've thought about, and dreamed about our being together as lovers. Both times, thirty years apart, when we spent nights together were wonderful, but then you broke my heart and kicked me aside. I still love you like no other woman I've ever known. I'll always love you, but I won't take another chance on you really wanting me in your life. I'm too old and tired to take a risk like that." Did he really say that, to Lydia? What was he doing? He wasn't sure.

"Kavanagh, I know you're tired. You've been working non-stop for me since you came to the hospital that day and saw me battered and broken. I know I don't look so good now, but I'm getting better and feeling better all the time. I thought we could go to Mexico to my place in Akumal for a while and start over, pretend it's the first time we've been there together. We'll go to that little outdoor restaurant with the Hurricane cocktails and music playing all night. I'll wear a yellow dress like the last time we were there. We'll make love on the beach at night and anywhere else you want to."

He couldn't believe what Lydia had offered. She offered to be the woman in his life, something he had desired for more than half his lifetime. Every night for so many years, before he slept, he imagined Lydia and him together. She was offering to give him what he wanted from her, lover, companion perhaps even marriage. How could he refuse her? He never refused Lydia anything she wanted when she asked. Somehow he summoned up the courage he needed. Kavanagh surprising himself, said, "Look Lydia, I'm going to California in a few days for a few days. When I get back, I'll get in touch with you or you can call anytime. We'll get together and talk about this. I have to say, I'm surprised, but I'm sure you'll be all right now."

Lydia was disappointed when she received a text from Kavanagh a week later. He said he was staying in California longer than he had intended and would talk with her when he returned to New York. What did brighten her mood was a news report that a man had somehow entered the top of the mammoth Ocean Wonders exhibit at the Coney Island Aquarium. While horrified spectators watched, the man struggled to climb out of the water. He wasn't able to escape and was torn apart by sharks representing the eighteen varieties of the deadly species housed in the three-story tank. Later, he was identified as Benni Zaiter, CEO of the dynamic company Amerind Botanical that had recently won the contract to supply 80% of the medicines for the entire Medicare program.

THE END